Hooking Up

by

Jessica L. Degarmo

ISBN   1461141400

EAN   978-1461141402

All rights reserved. No part of this book may be reproduced or transmitted in any form or by any means, electronic or mechanical, including photocopying, recording, or by any information storage and retrieval system, without permission in writing from the copyright owner.

'Hooking Up' was first published by Night Publishing, a trading name of Valley Strategies Ltd., a UK-registered private limited-liability company, registration number 5796186. Night Publishing can be contacted at: http://www.nightpublishing.com.

'Hooking Up' is the copyright of the author, Jessica L. Degarmo, 2011. All rights are reserved.

All characters are fictional, and any resemblance to anyone living or dead is accidental.

To my real family. You know who you are.

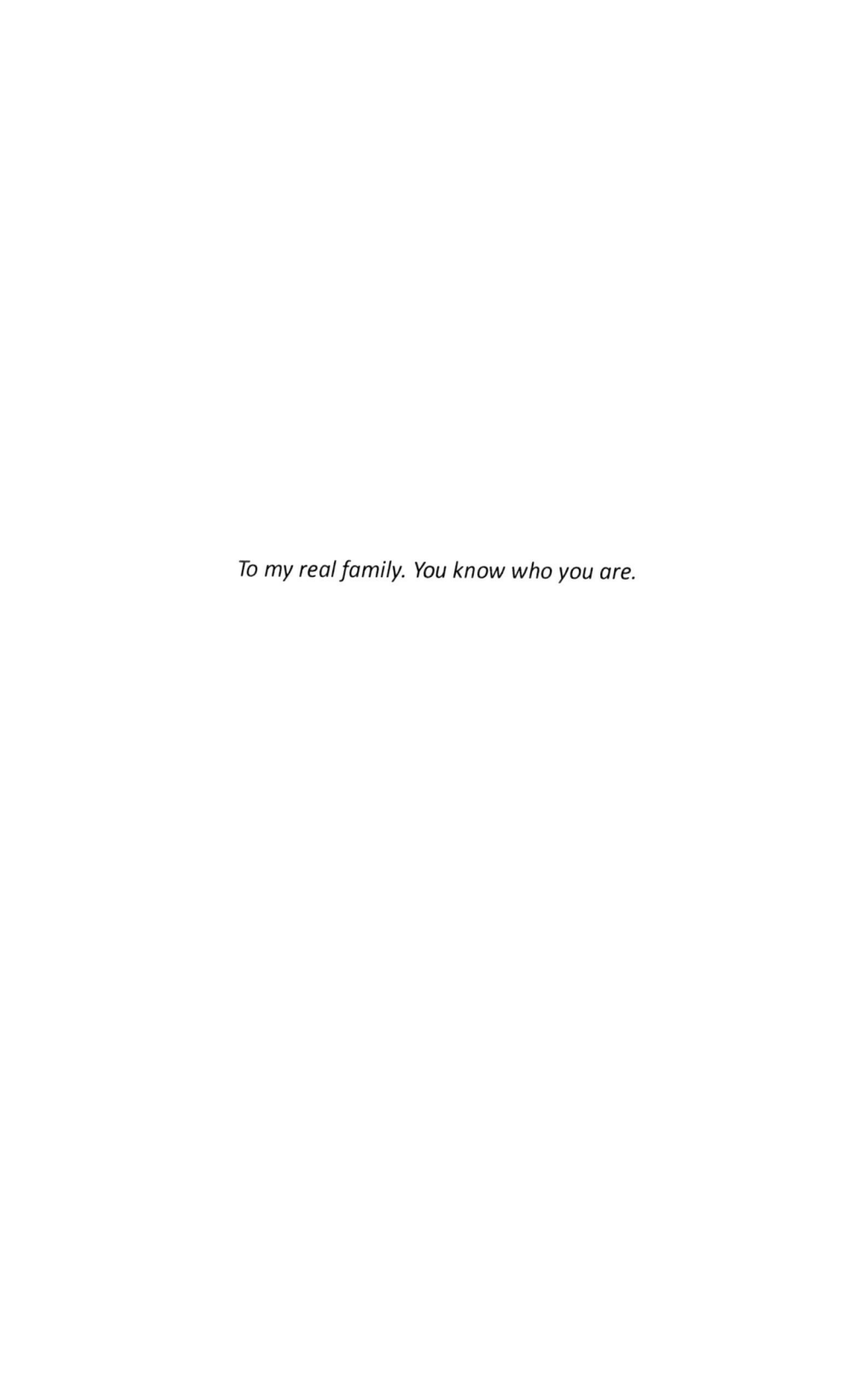

Chapter 1

Michael hefted the last box and set it outside our apartment door. He turned in the doorway and looked at me with that crooked grin that used to melt my heart. Well, it still melted my heart, but I had to learn to become unaffected by it.

It wasn't a fight or a sudden explosive episode that prompted our break-up, rather it was a gradual parting of ways that started perhaps as long as two years ago. Michael and I drifted apart as slowly as the continents, until at last we were oceans apart.

Michael was a great guy but, apparently, I didn't really do it for him anymore. He compared our relationship to an old sweatshirt: it fit and it was comfortable, but full of holes and stains. Eventually, as much as you liked the sweatshirt, it was time to get rid of it and buy a new spring wardrobe. So, he shucked me off like he shucked off his winter clothes, and he was ready to start over. He told me just last week, and by then he had already signed a lease on a new apartment. He was moving out at that very minute, leaving me behind, stunned and bewildered.

"I think that's the last of it," he said, trading his grin for a somber expression.

"Are you sure you want to do this?" I asked him. "Why don't you stay? We can talk."

"Caitlin, the time for talking is long past. Don't do this right now, please? I want to leave on a good note." He sighed.

"You're leaving me. There is no good note about it. Damn it, Michael. Why can't we just start over?" My voice rose, panic seeping in. He couldn't leave me. He just couldn't.

"Catie, it's done. We're done. Don't make this harder than it has to be." He glared at me angrily. It hurt. This rejection hurt. I was being abandoned.

He must have seen my growing hysteria, because he leaned against the door frame and said softly, "Do you think you'll be ok, Catie?"

"I'll be fine. Just—don't worry about me, alright? I'm tough. I can handle things."

"I always worry about you. I always will. You're my best friend."

"So why do you have to do this?" I asked plaintively.

"Because we grew up. We grew apart. You need something I can't give you anymore. Listen, I've got to go. I'll talk to you soon, ok?"

I sobbed once and turned from him so I didn't have to see him walk away. Once I heard the click of the door, I threw myself down on the floor and bawled like a baby. Unwillingly I was pulled back into another departure from my past.

'Caitlin, your parents' plane went down. There were no survivors."

Oh, God. Why did everyone always leave me?

It felt like hours before I could get up. The sun of the afternoon had given way to dusk and the dark suited my mood. I finally managed to prop myself up against the door and once upright, wiped my damp eyes on the bottom of my shirt. As much as I wanted to wallow in self-pity, I knew I couldn't. I had to pick myself up or else I never would. I did the only thing I could think of to take my mind off my troubles: I called my two best friends and arranged to meet them downtown.

So, here I was at a bar with my friends, single for the first time in ten years. It was Kelly's idea to come to the bar. She had just lost her job and she wanted a pick-me-up. I supposed that losing a topless dancing job would be heartbreaking to someone with her epic proportions and propensity for wiggling and jiggling. She seemed sultry even sitting still, elbows propped on the table, her face in her hands. She was good at her job but she had been replaced with a younger model.

"But I was so much better than that young little upstart. Her boobs aren't even real!" she whined, hanging her head in misery. "I have a much better routine than she does. All she does is twirl around a pole. I even have props, a real experience."

Her routine consisted of a rubber chicken, a farm-girl look complete with a straw hat, Daisy Dukes, a red-and-white checked button-down shirt that was tied around her midriff (while it was on), and a painfully affected Southern drawl. I'm not going to mention what she did with the chicken. It was nice to have ambition, however, and I sympathized with my friend.

"She'll probably waste away after the first month, and then they'll call you and beg you to come back. Besides, you're too good for them. What about the place over town? Boobz N' Booze?" I asked, rubbing her back through her tight leather bodysuit.

She shook her head. "I already tried. They said they were full, but they'd call if something came up. What am I going to do? How am I going to pay for school if I don't have a job?" she wailed.

It just goes to show you that looks aren't everything. Besides having a bodacious bod, Kelly was a whiz. She was smarter than anyone else I knew, and she had wanted to be a lawyer for as long as I'd known her. She'd been putting herself through law school and she was only a year away from graduating. I knew she'd find a way to make things work for her, but until then she was entitled to a little bit of self-pity. By tomorrow she'd be up and scheming again.

"To having options!" I toasted, trying to make Kelly feel better.

"Catie, where were you just a minute ago? You seemed miles away," Heidi said, gently shaking my arm. Heidi was the more sensitive member of our group, young, idealistic, and a virgin. When she first moved to the city from her small hometown in Illinois, she tried to go wild but, unfortunately, volunteering at church and feeding the homeless don't really help a bad-girl image. I smiled at her and pulled myself back into their conversation after I realized that neither of them knew that Michael and I ended things.

"I need to tell you something," I said, looking at both of them sheepishly.

"What?" Kelly asked, her smooth brow rumpling a little as she looked at me.

"So, tell us now," Heidi urged.

I took a deep breath. "It's over between Michael and me. He signed a lease on an apartment on the East side and he moved out today. That's really why I wanted to go out tonight, to get my mind off things."

The bar was suddenly filled with shrew-like shrieks and distressed feminine wails. They even drowned out the jukebox.

"What?" Heidi yelled. "Why didn't you say something earlier, you moron?"

"Well, that trumps me losing my job! What the hell?" Kelly hollered.

I shushed them both quickly. The old men at the bar were starting to stare. "I just didn't want to get into it, that's all. Sorry."

They both looked at me like I was crazy. "How could you not want to talk about breaking up with your boyfriend?" Heidi accused skeptically. "This is big. How do you feel?"

"I'm fine. It's not a big deal, really. It's been coming for a long time, guys," I told them, shrugging my shoulders, hiding the pain under a guise of nonchalance. "No problems. Just done and over with."

"But why?" asked Kelly, sounding concerned now that the initial shock had passed. Even though Kelly and Heidi were my best friends, I didn't tell them everything. A girl needed to keep some things to herself. I had never been one for girl-talk, and I certainly didn't want them to know that I was such a loser that I couldn't keep a man.

"It just happened. These things do. It was time for both of us to move on. So now I'm a free agent." A free agent? What does that even *mean*? I was resorting to pulling out sports analogies? Great.

"You know what you need now?" Heidi, our innocent friend, asked. "You need a hook-up."

Kelly choked on her drink and I gaped, my jaw falling almost to the floor. I pounded Kelly on the back to help her stop choking and silently repeated Heidi's completely unexpected idea. A hook-up?

Chapter 2

Kelly recovered first. "Ok, explain yourself," she demanded, wiping her mouth with her napkin and giggling.

Heidi beamed. "It's simple. You just got out of a serious relationship, so now you need to have a hook-up to get over Michael and move on." She looked proud of herself. "I read it in a magazine."

I burst into laughter. "How do you propose that I *hook up*?" Something like this coming from Heidi was like hearing Santa Claus swearing—it was completely out of character.

"Well, you find a cute guy, go up to him and ask him to sleep with you, and then you do it." She was actually serious. Heidi, pure as the driven snow and destined to remain that way until she tied the knot with some good, corn-fed boy, was serious about me finding a random guy to have sex with.

Kelly must have had the same thought I did because she started laughing so hard she snorted. Eventually she caught her breath, rolled her eyes and said to Heidi, "Where is she supposed to meet this cute guy? And what about disease and creepy stalkers and pregnancy?"

"Well, use a condom, hook up in a neutral place, and make sure to take the morning-after pill. That's what the article said," Heidi said indignantly.

I didn't know what to say. A hook-up? With some random guy? How does one even begin to prepare for that, much less do it? What would I do—just walk up to some random guy, say, "Hey, baby, are you looking for a good time?" and run off to the parking lot and do it in a car? How yucky. I shrugged off the thought and concentrated instead on my screwdriver.

"Heidi, you wild woman, I think I'll pass. But thanks," I said, giving her a one-armed hug.

Kelly and Heidi laughed, and we all pounded our drinks. It was really just what I needed and I felt myself relaxing from more than the alcohol. I had my two best friends in the world, our familiar home pub, and the men were starting to line up to liquor us up. What more did a girl need?

I watched my two best friends get silly on screwdrivers and flirt with the old men at the bar and I helped them to the restroom when they needed to go. Neither of my girls could hold their liquor and, as always, I ended up taking care of them, not that I minded. I had always been more level-headed than Kelly and earthier than Heidi. We danced to the corny '80s music blasting from the jukebox and giggled when the old men tried to keep up. I felt good. As long as I didn't dwell on my empty apartment, my empty bed, my empty heart.

By midnight, both girls were sloppy, and I peeled them off their barstools and called them a cab. I walked home, relishing the crisp evening air on my overheated skin. I wasn't worried about anyone bothering me. Although I was considered slender at 5'7" and 120 lbs., I had always been able to take care of myself. I earned a brown belt in karate and felt confident that I could handle an attacker. Besides, I had lived in this town my whole life and the only exciting thing that ever happened in my twenty-eight years was when the old pavilion in the outskirts of town was burned to the ground by some local hoodlums.

Letting myself into a dark apartment was new. Since Michael's things had been moved out, the place looked bare and sterile. The furnishings that were left seemed forlorn and miniscule in the large space. I threw my purse on the kitchen counter, flicked on the light to the living room in passing, and kicked off my shoes. I left them on the rug, shiny mementos of a happy time, and headed to my bedroom. At least I still had my bed. Michael had taken our couch and left me with only an armchair and a single end table in the living room. The rest of the furniture, including the TV and the entertainment stand, had been moved to the apartment on the East side.

As I slid out of my dress and hung it up in the now half-empty closet, I thought of Michael. How was he doing? Did he miss me? Did I miss him?

I did. There was something unsettling about coming home to a quiet place. Michael was heavily into sports and music, and he always cranked the volume on the TV or the stereo when he was home. I had come home from work and gotten a headache simply by walking inside the apartment more than once over the past ten years. But at least someone was there. The place was silent now, and for once I had room to think, to rest, to just be. It was a somber change, and an unwelcome one. Who wants to just *be*?

I crawled into bed and buried my head in his pillow, inhaling deeply. He always wore the nicest cologne. I wondered why he hadn't taken his pillow. Maybe he bought new ones. Maybe he didn't want to chance smelling my perfume in his dreams. Maybe he was trying to erase any evidence that I had ever been present in his bed. I wouldn't blame him. Ten years was a long time to spend with someone, and since we ended things, the time seemed somehow wasted.

I got up and stripped the sheets from the bed. I rummaged through the closet until I found a new, scent-free set, and remade the bed. Crawling in again, I sniffed. Satisfied that there was no longer a trace of Michael, I sighed and fell asleep.

The next morning was equally quiet. I didn't wake up to the sound of Michael humming in the bathroom, and I didn't have to make eggs for two. I could read the newspaper as slowly as I wanted without worrying that I was taking too long with the sports section. I didn't have to share the bathroom, the toaster or the coffeepot. This was ok. Really. Maybe If I kept thinking this way, I'd eventually convince myself.

I refused to acknowledge the emptiness that was nestled deep inside me and building like a malignant growth. I refused to let myself wallow in self-recrimination or pity, and I refused to miss Michael.

After breakfast, I decided to rearrange my pitiful collection of furniture throughout the apartment. I pushed the bed to the opposite wall, moved my dresser closer to the bathroom door, and hefted the bookshelf in our room until it was next to the side of the bed that Michael always occupied. I grabbed a spare comforter and put it on the bed, just to change the look. I stepped back, perused the now completely different room, and nodded. I moved to the living room and, since I only had an armchair and an end table, did nothing. I guessed that I would have to go shopping soon for something to fill the space. It was too bad that I couldn't do the same for myself. I had a lot of empty space to fill.

Satisfied with my efforts, I hopped in the shower and scrubbed the scent of used tobacco from the night before from my skin. I pulled on some sweats and an old holey t-shirt and sat down to think.

It's funny how some ideas, although they are completely crazy and not worth even an iota of thought, can stick with you. Though Kelly and I laughed at Heidi's magazine idea, it was stuck in my craw and stuck good. A hook-up sounded dangerous, and actually kind of slutty, but maybe it was the right thing to do. People have rebound relationships all the time and they are no worse for wear afterward. But could I do it? I had never had a one-night stand. As a matter of fact, Michael was my first, and only, serious relationship, pathetic as that seemed in such sexually enlightened times.

Michael and I had known each other since grade school. He was the first person besides my immediate family who heard the news that my parents died in a plane crash. He was there for me and held my hand and acted as my rock more times than I could count. We attended high school together and we drifted together romantically in much the same way we eventually drifted apart—slowly. We were always in the same group of friends and, one night, when we were the last two of our group to be walking home from the movies together, we kissed. It had been sweet, chaste, and just the sort of thing that shy teenagers would do. Neither of us had any idea of what to do about the budding attraction we felt for each other. We groped like the gawky teenagers we were in the back of his car, we walked to classes together, and we went to senior prom together. And that night, after prom, we consummated our romance in a hotel room he reserved for the occasion. We never imagined that we'd be anything other than together. It was a comfortable relationship from the start, aided by the fact that we had grown up together. So when had we grown apart?

I was old-fashioned by nature. I was never promiscuous and I had never thought of having sex just for the sake of having sex. It was supposed to mean something. With Michael, it had meant something. But here I was, seriously contemplating having a one-night stand with some random stranger who meant absolutely nothing to me, and to whom I meant absolutely nothing. That was wrong, right?

I wasn't so sure. Everything else had changed so drastically in such a short time. Why couldn't I? I felt like I had to do something, anything to take my mind off my loneliness.

The only person I could call to help me with such a radical

change of self, besides Michael, was Kelly. Kelly was my co-conspirator in everything. We had gotten in a lot of trouble throughout the years. She was the only person I would ever even consider talking with about taking such a drastic measure. She would tell it to me straight.

"Catie, you can't be serious!" she exclaimed, and I was sure that on the other end of the phone line she was throwing her hand up in the air in a gesture of futility. "You? The Queen of the Prudes?"

I took offense to that remark. I wasn't a prude. I was just ... controlled. Sorry if I didn't undress in front of thirty guys every night for tips. I preferred a more subtle approach. I frowned. Seriously, what did my friends think of me?

"I just think that maybe I need something different. I've never just gone out and done it before. Maybe it's time to experience what every other girl in the United States experienced when she was a teenager."

"I just think that Heidi was way off-base with the whole hook-up thing. You never know what you'll run into out there. I think you can do better."

"But it hurts. This loneliness thing hurts. I don't like it." I was dangerously close to whimpering, something completely unlike me.

"You won't be happy with yourself afterward, you know. That

type of behavior is not in your makeup. I'm surprised you're even considering it. You don't want to do this. Really you don't. You just want something. Take my advice, and let it be for now. You'll feel differently in a month or two, I swear."

"You're probably right," I conceded. After all, I had just gotten out of a relationship. I didn't need any complications right now. I had to find myself, that's all. I couldn't rely on a guy to find me for me. And why, for Pete's sake, was I contemplating dating advice from a twenty-three-year-old virgin who swore up and down the first time she would do the good old up and down would be on her wedding night? I would be much better off listening to the stripper.

So, I forgot about it. I would concentrate on finding me and leave the rest to fate. How hard could that be?

Chapter 3

After another rough night of missing Michael, I decided to call my grandmother, not for support really, but because I thought I should. She raised me after my parents died, but she didn't like it, and she normally never approved of the choices I made. Actually, there wasn't much about me that she liked. Period. Surprisingly, however, Gran always liked Michael. I had been dreading telling her that he dumped me ever since it happened. I knew she would blame me somehow.

I settled myself on my bed and took a deep breath, sighed and dialed.

Her cultured voice sounded slightly irritated when she answered the phone. I glanced at the clock and groaned to myself. 6:30? Great—right in the middle of her nightly news program. Amelia Danforth, my blue-blooded Gran (and don't ever call her Millie) hated to be interrupted during her TV shows. Strike one.

"Hi, Gran. It's me. How are you?"

"Fine, Caitlin. Just watching the news. What are you doing?"

"Nothing, really. Can I talk to you for a minute?"

"You are, aren't you?"

Yes, she was irritated. And she was already making me feel like a wayward child instead of a twenty-eight-year-old woman.

"Yes, sorry. Listen, I just wanted to tell you that Michael and I aren't together anymore. He moved out a few days ago."

"What? Whatever for? What did you do?"

I guess I shouldn't have expected any less. Still, it hurt.

"Gran, it wasn't like that. We just grew apart. He decided he needed his space, so I let him go. End of story. Nothing happened and I didn't *do* anything."

"Well, you must have done something. Nice boys just don't walk away and leave their girlfriends of ten years. Did you ask him what you did to make him want to leave?"

"Yes, Gran. I did. He said that he didn't like the way I made toast in the morning, so he left. There—happy now?" Strike two. Catie, don't lose your cool. But some things just don't change and I could feel the age-old fight brewing.

"Well, you don't have to be rude. I'm just saying that you should really look inside yourself to figure out why he would want to leave you, then fix it so you can get him back."

"Ok, Gran. I'll do that. And while I'm at it, I'll look into that whole global warming thing. Maybe since I'm directly responsible for the core temperature of the earth rising, I'll find a way to fix that too. What do you think?"

"You know I don't appreciate your sarcasm when I'm simply trying to help. I don't see why you have to fling my advice back into my face when I'm just being supportive. It's not becoming, you know, and I raised you better than that. Nice girls don't mouth off to their grandmothers." Strike three. The guilt trip. I needed to hang up or I'd end up screaming at her.

"Well, I'll let you get back to your show. Sorry to bother you."

"Alright, dear. I'll talk to you soon." She hung up the phone and I flopped back onto my bed in exasperation. As frenetic as my life was at this moment, some things remained constant.

It had always been this way between me and my grandmother. When I was younger, she'd try everything she could to control me and mold me into what she thought I should be. I was admonished constantly to stand up straight and suck in my stomach, wear more mascara and dress more like a girl. She wanted me to be a ballerina and refused to attend my karate tournaments because she thought it was too unladylike. She constantly criticized what I did.

The very week we graduated from high school, Michael and I signed a lease on an apartment across town just to get away from her. I could only handle her and her sharp tongue with its pointed barbs in small doses. I compared our relationship to the lab rat experiments that scientists used to perform. After a while, the rats won't grab the cheese if they get electrocuted enough. I was the rat and Gran was the Muenster. I was sick of getting stung. As a result of her constant criticism, I rarely went to see her anymore. I wasn't sure why I even called her for support because she never gave any. I blamed myself for expecting something different. Oh well, live and learn, I supposed.

Being alone sucked, but it was better than being with Gran. Sighing, I boosted myself off the bed and headed for the kitchen. There was no point in rehashing the past and, besides, there was a pint of Chunky Monkey with my name all over it.

My solitary confinement continued over the next two months. I pretended to concentrate on being happy single. I had to find some way to cope with the loneliness that threatened to swallow me whole. I stared in the mirror and repeated a mantra I created: I, Caitlin Paige Edison, am unattached and proud. I am independent and strong. I don't need a man to complete me. I am intelligent, beautiful and competent.

I went through the motions of being a confident single woman every day, never acknowledging that I was missing something. I didn't call my grandmother, and when she finally remembered that she had a granddaughter and tried to call me, I contrived countless excuses to avoid lengthy conversations with her. I couldn't handle any more blows to my already fragile self-esteem. So, for all she knew, I was out and about constantly, filling my day with so many activities that I barely had a moment. In reality, I went to work, came home, cooked for one or ordered a small takeout meal, and burrowed in my apartment like a mole. I stopped going out with my girls because they gave me pitying looks and tried to set me up with guys they knew. I wasn't interested. I was far too busy finding myself. They eventually quit trying to set me up, and I was glad. I just wanted to be alone.

But something was missing, and the shit hit the fan one day in February—February fourteenth, to be exact.

Chapter 4

I woke up grumpy but I didn't know why. I honestly didn't even realize what day it was until I glanced at the calendar hanging innocuously on the fridge. It was Valentine's Day, and I was alone. My Lucky Charms weren't sweet enough to take the bitter taste of being alone on a lover's holiday off the tip of my tongue. I was alone. Michael always did something for me on Valentine's Day, and he never even needed prompting. He usually brought me flowers and chocolates and took me to dinner, and I realized with a start that there was nothing awaiting me today. No surprise deliveries, no sweet treats, no paid-for romantic repasts. There was just an empty apartment, an empty datebook, and me, empty inside.

Did Michael really mean that much, or was it just the relationship that mattered? I wondered what he was doing, and briefly thought about calling him. My hand hovered over the phone but, after a second, I dropped it to my side in a fit of temper. Sometimes I disgusted myself. I had to let him go.

But I missed all the courting rituals, the sweet foreplay that preceded romantic sex. I missed having a man.

Throughout the day my mind was not on my work. My job as a pediatric physical therapist was usually rewarding, but today all I could think of was my own form of therapy. I felt the need for contact as sharply as I would feel a needle in my side. It poked at me all day, bruising and piercing my tender flesh. I needed a connection badly.

After work I drove by the fancy restaurants that Michael used to take me to. They were all crowded with couples. I stopped my car outside my favorite, Les Deux, and gazed into the windows. The happy couples seated inside looked blissful. Though I couldn't hear the conversations, I knew how they went: 'I love you. I love you more.'

I hurried back to my car in shame. What was wrong with me? Had I really pressed my face against the glass of a restaurant and imagined myself among the happy couples?

When I got back to my apartment, I was struck again by Heidi's words. Suddenly, they didn't seem so ludicrous. Why not find someone to ease the pain with? Who said that I had to be in love with the guy I was sleeping with? Maybe a good roll was all I needed to make me less lonely. After all, I was an adult. I had needs and I was prepared to deal with the consequences of my actions. I was willing to try anything that would take away the ache that had become a burning pyre inside my body. Something was seriously missing, and I aimed to find it.

Having decided to launch a full-scale manhunt, I dressed with care. I wanted to accentuate my long legs and slim waist. A black tank-dress suited my mood well. Underneath, I wore a lacy black thong and a push-up bra.

I fussed with my hair, finally letting it sweep over my shoulders in dark waves. I could never do anything with it anyway. I applied my makeup carefully, accenting my eyes. Finally I spritzed on Red Door, my favorite perfume. It always made me feel very powerful and sexy. I slid my feet into ankle-breaking stilettos and perused myself in my full-length mirror. I was ready. For what, I didn't know. I took a deep breath and headed to my car.

I drove around town aimlessly. I didn't know who or what I was looking for. All I knew was that there was someone out there who would fall for my charms, and I would take advantage of him. I didn't exactly feel good about that, but I didn't feel good about staying home and crying my lonely self to sleep either. Which was the lesser of two evils? I had no idea.

I pulled up alongside a decent-looking bar called The Wave. It was well-lit and meticulously maintained. There were no creepy-looking drunks hanging around outside. Instead, the brick storefront featured flashing neon signs advertising Bud and Miller. Cheery curtains hung in the front windows. How bad could a guy be in such a place, I wondered, and parked my car.

I ventured inside, glancing left then right casually, but with the full-alertness of a veteran karate brown-belt. I would know what I was getting myself into.

I didn't see any amazing guys straight-off. Rather, they all seemed to blend into one big pool of potential. A few glanced in my direction and quickly looked away, almost as though they were afraid of offending me. On the one night I wanted to be noticed, guys were being respectful? What—no catcalls, wolf-whistles, or rude gestures? It was almost laughable, but I didn't feel like laughing.

I found a small table adjacent to the bar and sat with my back to the wall. I debated leaving after about five minutes, but I have never been one to run away from anything. I always faced my problems and my attackers with equal zest. I would win this night, no matter what it took.

I placed an order with the roving waitress for a vodka martini. I wanted to appear confident, in-control, and sexy, and I knew of no other drink that would allow me to look that way. The vodka martini was a symbol. It said, "Come get me boys—I'm all yours."

When I received my drink, I sipped it slowly and gazed over the rim at the individual tables where patrons of all shapes and sizes sat, engaged in earnest drinking or earnest conversation. There were a few really hot guys at some of the tables, but the numbers intimidated me. I didn't feel like separating a guy from his bunch of buddies. I allowed my gaze to wander further and I was rewarded with the sight of a lone man sitting in the far corner of the room, nursing a beer with a thoughtful look on his face while he watched the flat screen on the wall. He was tall, judging by the way he filled out the stool, his knees bent and his feet resting on the lowermost rung of the bar stool, and his short dark hair was carelessly styled. He had dark eyes too, and an olive complexion. He was perfect.

I always liked tall, dark and handsome. Michael was an odd choice for me, having both blond hair and blue eyes, but I never really minded. Now, my mouth watered in anticipation. I couldn't believe my own reaction to a stranger, but the pull was gravitational.

I eased myself off my bar stool and carried my drink over to his table. I lowered my eyelids and peered at him with a smoky gaze. "Do you mind if I join you?"

He looked up at me, startled, then said in a mellow voice, "Sure. Help yourself."

I slid into the seat across from him, toyed with the stem of my glass and asked, "Do you come here often?" I couldn't believe such drivel had escaped my lips, but he didn't seem to notice the tired come-on.

"No, first time. You?" His voice was pleasant, deep, and seductive. I felt myself getting antsy. I wanted to grab his hand and lead him out the door. The want was excruciating.

"First time for me, too. Do you believe in fate?" I asked him in a husky voice, my violet eyes probing his black ones.

He colored. "Yeah, I guess I do."

Someone loaded the jukebox and music started playing. It was slow and sweet. He cleared his throat and asked, "Would you like to dance?"

I nodded and he took my hand, leading me to the center of the room to the makeshift dance floor. He wrapped his arms around my waist. The contact was so sweet that I wanted to moan. It had been too long. It felt so good to be held. If I closed my eyes, I could almost imagine that we were a couple, and this wasn't just a chance meeting in a bar. Maybe imagining things that way would make this blatant seduction easier. I wound my arms around his neck and moved closer to him, resting my head on his shoulder. He smelled edible. I melted into him and tried to make my intentions clear.

He murmured something unintelligible and pulled me even closer. He must have understood. The music wrapped us in its sensual melody. The drums and the bass throbbed, and as they did, so did I.

"What's your name?"

"Caitlin. What's yours?"

"Ryan," he answered, squeezing me once. I groaned and nuzzled his neck. The way he smelled should be illegal. It was like a drug, drawing me closer, addicting me, and making me crave things that I probably shouldn't. Out-of-character things.

When the dance ended, he made as if to release me. I wouldn't allow it. I kept my arms wrapped around his neck and tilted my head up to his. I brushed my lips against his cheek and asked him, "Do you want to get out of here?"

I was amazed at how easy it was to be wanton. The way that I felt right now was anything but innocent, and I couldn't believe it was actually me, there with him, doing things no good girl ever does. But tonight, all thoughts of good and bad flew out of my head. I was going with my instincts. I needed this like a parched traveler needed water, like an addict needed her drug of choice.

He nodded to me and grabbed my hand. We raced outside but paused on the sidewalk outside the bar. The dilemma became obvious: what did we do now? Rent a hotel room? I only had twenty bucks on me.

"Well, what would you like to do now?" he asked me, gazing at me sensuously.

Did I dare go to his place? After all, I didn't know him, although I would shortly. The need was unbearable. I made my decision.

"My place is nearby. Come on, I know what we can do," I told him, grinding against him sensuously. He nodded again and I led him to my car.

I drove home quickly, very aware of the stranger's hand rubbing my thigh gently. There was no way I should be doing this right now, but I didn't care. I had to fill the emptiness somehow, and there was no turning back. We didn't speak, but no words were necessary.

I parked and he came around to my side of the car to open my door for me. He lifted me out of the car and wrapped his arms around my waist, pulling me toward him. He backed me up against the side of my car and flattened his hips against me, arms winding around my midsection, his hands sliding up and down my back in a titillating rhythm. His lips found mine and there was nothing innocent or shy about them. The pressure of his lips on mine was seductive, maddening. Simultaneously, we moaned and his fingers threaded through my hair, pulling a little as he directed my mouth to where he wanted it. He deepened this kiss quickly, his tongue tangling with mine in a full-out erotic caress that was mind-blowing. I was lost immediately. The kiss continued for about a minute until I realized where we were and what we were doing.

I made a little desperate sound in my throat and broke the kiss urgently. I shoved at him so I could move, grabbed his hand and pulled him up the stairs toward my apartment door. I fumbled with the lock as his hand fumbled with my dress and I practically yanked him inside.

Even after so many years with Michael, I never felt this level of passion with him, but this dark stranger incited fires in my bloodstream. He stroked my shoulders, my sides, my waist, finally moving his hands up to caress my breasts through the thin silk. I moaned again and pushed the straps of my dress off my shoulders. He peeled it down to my waist and bent to press warm, wet kisses onto my neck and the curve of my bosom. My hands tangled in his hair. His arms encircled me and I felt him struggle with my bra as he tried to unbuckle it. He succeeded and, when my breasts were free, he groaned and feasted on them. I undid the buttons on his shirt and ran my hands down the smooth, solid warmth of his chest. He was firmly muscled and lean, and taller than me, which was a bonus. As he nuzzled me senseless, I attached my lips first to his neck and then to his ear and drew forth little groans of delight from my lover. Our clothes seemed to fall off like magic.

I led him to my bedroom and pushed him down onto the bed. I

stretched out on top of him and marveled at the solid warmth beneath me. He rolled us over and shifted so that he was nestled between my thighs. He ravished my neck, my ear, my shoulder, then lower, lower. I gasped recklessly, completely lost in passion. When he entered me, I arched and moaned like I was being electrocuted. As he moved, he murmured soft words in my ear, his breath warming my neck and sending shivers up and down my spine. His voice was just as erotic as the motion of our entangled bodies. Within minutes, he had me screaming.

For the next two hours, we enjoyed each other. We gorged ourselves on the other's skin, drowning in the smell, the feel, the taste of each other. Finally, we lay exhausted and satisfied in each other's arms. I snuggled against him and sighed, feeling very sated and sleepy, but with a jolt, I realized that I had a problem. How did I get rid of him?

Chapter 5

I had fallen asleep against my better judgment and the only thought I had upon waking was, "Oh, God, I hope he's gone." No such luck. Next to me was a warm, sexy, sleeping male, and I had no idea what to do about it. Heidi's plan didn't mention anything about what to do if your one-night stand stays over. I wasn't sure I even remembered his name. Ron, Randy, Ryan? Oh—right, Ryan.

I eased myself off of the mattress, trying not to wake him. I found my bathrobe and shrugged into it. Maybe if I simply avoided him, he'd get up and leave. If not, I could always pretend like I had something very important to do and usher him out the door. I could give him a bad phone number, or move, or dye my hair so he wouldn't know it was me….

He snuffed once, yawned, and rolled over. His long, muscular arms reached over his head as he stretched. He cleared his throat—a deep, masculine sound—and opened his eyes, peering at me out of sleep-weighted lids. "Where are you going?" he inquired, grinning at me winsomely.

"I just, uh, I have to, you know, things to do—" I stammered, completely at a loss for words.

"Mmmm," he murmured drowsily, "I slept like the dead." He got up, and oh dear Lord, he was completely naked. Apparently, my passion-filled brain hadn't exaggerated his assets. He was gorgeous. But how did I get rid of him? The last thing I wanted to do was to get messed up with some random guy after coming out of a serious relationship. But how did I tell him that? Damn me and my wayward hormones! Why, oh why, had I acted on Heidi's lame-brained idea?

"Listen, Ryan, you were great and all, but I really have someplace I need to be," I told him, trying to sound apologetic. "Do you want me to call you a cab?"

"No, that's ok. I'll just show myself out. I don't live that far from here anyway," he said, finally pulling his boxer shorts and jeans on. His stomach muscles rippled with the effort and my jaw went slack. This was a fine specimen of male, and I felt myself go soft and melty again as I thought of the magic he had worked on me the night before. I could still feel his arms around me and the surprising tenderness of his touch. No getting gooey over the one-night stand, I admonished myself furiously. It was over.

"Ok. Well, thanks," I said, coloring. Did I actually just thank the random guy that screwed my brains out last night? Was that appropriate? Oh, how awkward this was becoming

"Yeah. Thank you. I guess I'll call you later?"

I figured that something in my face must have revealed my

reluctance to turn this into anything other than a hook-up because he shrugged, grabbed his shoes, slid them on, and bundled himself into the jacket that had been carelessly flung across the room the night before in the throes of passion.

I jotted down a bad phone number, handed it to him, and walked him to the door. He paused in the door frame and leaned toward me. Touching his cheek to mine, he whispered, "Good morning, Caitlin," and gave me a sweet, tender kiss on the lips. He walked backwards out of the door, maintaining eye contact the whole time, and finally turned around and sprinted down the stairs to the sidewalk. I gently shut the door and locked it.

Well, I had done it. I hooked up to make myself feel sexy, independent and whole. I found a random guy to share my bed for the night and kicked him out at dawn. This was supposed to make me feel better, so why didn't it?

I felt sexually fulfilled but the emptiness was still there. I felt like a person who was dying for water. One sip eased the acute pain, but the intense thirst remained. What the hell? I should have borrowed Heidi's copy of that damned magazine instead of getting my information second-hand.

I showered frantically and tried to remove the scent of the seductive stranger from my skin. Every pore in my sex-starved body burned again as I remembered his touch. He was a skillful lover and I briefly thought it was too bad that he was destined to be just a passing notch on my bedpost. After I felt clean again, I decided to call Heidi. I wanted the scoop on the rest of the article.

Heidi picked up on the third ring. She sounded like she had been sleeping and, with one glance at my living room clock, I knew why. It was only eight in the morning. I had awoken unusually early following my tryst and I simply didn't think to look at the time before I called. My internal clock was all screwed up. Literally.

"Heidi, it's me. Sorry to wake you," I apologized. "Do you want me to call you later?"

"No, that's ok. I had to get up anyway to get to the soup kitchen in time to start making lunch. What's up?"

I took a deep breath. "Hey, in that magazine article you read, what does it say about the morning after?"

"Oh, my God! You didn't! Tell me all about it!" I could picture her bolting upright in her bed, her blue eyes wide and eager as she quizzed me.

"No, I think I'll pass. Just tell me—what do I do now?" I asked, trying to settle more comfortably into my armchair. I still hadn't gotten any furniture and I made a mental note to find a couch. This chair was hard as a rock. Like Ryan's abs. Damn it.

"Well, you just go about your day-to-day business and forget you did it. Then good stuff is supposed to happen."

"Good stuff? Like what? I thought the sex was the good stuff," I said, frowning. What more could there be to this whole deal?

"Well, you're supposed to realize the power of your femininity and use it to make different choices. At least that's what that article says. You really did it? I can't believe you really did it!" She sounded impressed. I didn't know how to feel.

"Just forget I called, ok, Heidi? Go make soup." I regretted calling her. Before I knew it, she'd call Kelly and then they'd both come over and demand the play-by-play. I couldn't believe I did it, and I certainly wasn't going to talk about it. Even if it was the best sex I'd ever had (it was), I was not the kind to kiss and tell.

For the rest of the day, I tried to squash my regrets and focus on feeling the powerful femininity coursing through me. The problem was all I felt was irked and a little embarrassed. How could I have done such a thing? I really had to take up a hobby or something—anything to get my mind off my sexual frustration.

I raced around my apartment and cleaned like a whirling dervish. I washed and dried my sheets (no sense having a stranger's cologne linger on my pillow), dusted, polished all of the surfaces I could find, and vacuumed like I was possessed. Even so, the night before replayed itself in my mind, and I found myself holding my feather duster still in midair, aroused anew by my daydreaming. I shook my head to clear the visions and decided to clean harder, attacking my apartment with a vengeance.

I had just finished up when the doorbell rang. I ran to get it and looked through the peephole. It was him! Ryan had come back! What the hell for? Didn't he understand the phrase "one-night stand"? Christ, it had the words "one-night" in it! What did I do? And, crap, look what I was wearing!

The doorbell rang again and I had a sneaking suspicion he could see me through the other side of the peephole. Resigned, I patted down my unruly hair and answered the door.

He stood in the doorway, his broad shoulders almost touching both sides of the door frame, and he looked glorious. His dark hair was gleaming like he had just jumped out of the shower. The warm, masculine aroma wafting from his skin was enough to make my mouth water. *Down girl*, I reprimanded myself. He was just a one-night stand, remember? He wore his faded jeans well; they sat low on his hips. His navy blue t-shirt clung to the muscles on his arms and chest and made his complexion look even swarthier. My heart stuttered again as he gazed at me softly. His dark eyes glittered in the lamplight and, when he smiled at me, my heart gave one giant thump and stopped for just a fraction of a second. It was enough to alert me to the fact that I was smitten. But what did I do about it? This was not supposed to happen.

"Hey, Caitlin." He gazed at me solemnly and stepped forward. "Do you mind if I come in?"

I shrugged and backed up to let him in. The whole time, my frantic mind wondered, what is he doing here?

I swallowed and said, "What's up?"

He wandered further into the room and glanced at my lack of home furnishings. His brow wrinkled in thought as he asked, "Did you just move in here or something?"

"Or something," I told him. "So, uh, was there something you needed? I'm pretty busy, you know." I tried to keep my tone casual but firm, with no luck. My voice shook a little as I spoke.

He must have noticed my discomfort but he didn't say anything about it. Instead, he gestured to my forlorn little armchair and said, "Do you mind if I sit down?"

I minded, but didn't know how to say it without sounding like a royal bitch, so I gestured to the chair, "Help yourself."

He folded himself into the tiny chair and looked up at me. I had no choice but to stand because there was only one seat in the living room, and he was in it.

"Why did you give me a bad phone number?" he asked me earnestly.

"What? A bad number?" I stammered like a complete jackass. He was on to me and I had nothing to say for myself. Damn that magazine for publishing such a stupid article anyway. Sure—hook up with a guy, be powerful and feminine—I would have gladly choked the journalist who wrote that piece of crap.

"You know what I'm talking about. I want to know why you did it after such an incredible night."

He looked at me levelly, waiting for my response. I wasn't used to such a direct approach. Michael was always shy and non-confrontational. Any time something bothered him, he'd just hole himself up in our spare bedroom that he converted into a computer room and play games on his computer until either he felt better or he got up the nerve to talk to me. I think I intimidated him. No such luck here. Ryan was holding his own, or maybe even winning.

I decided to give it to him straight. "Listen, Ryan, you were great —last night was great—but I really don't need a relationship right now. I just got out of one and I don't think it's smart for me to get serious anytime soon. I'm sorry."

"Serious?" he questioned, snorting a little. "How can you possibly know if we could get serious without giving us a chance first?"

I was staggered. Did the man have an answer for everything?

I decided to try another, slightly cruder, tactic. "Ryan, I only wanted to hook up for one night. That's all. I never expected you to show up on my doorstep but I guess that's what I get for bringing you to my house." How could I have been so stupid? Damn hormones.

"Oh, I see. A one-night stand." He frowned, looking hurt. "Now I know how it feels."

"Listen, I'm sorry, ok? I didn't mean to, like, hurt you or anything. I thought that we'd just do the deed and move on. That's all. You're great, you really are, but I can't do more than that right now."

"Right now?" he said, picking up on the one phrase that he shouldn't have. "So, when?"

"That's not what I meant. I think you should go now, ok? Thanks for a good time, but this is good-bye."

I grasped his arm, willing myself not to notice how warm and muscular it was, and herded him toward the exit. He spun just as he reached the door, locking me in an embrace, which I struggled against futilely, kissed me quickly on the lips and said, "Not good-bye, just good-bye for now."

He turned on his heel and left me gaping in the doorway. Oh, crap. What did I do now? This was really not supposed to happen.

I went to Kelly's house after I calmed down and made sure that my stalker-lover, Ryan, had actually left the premises. Kelly was waiting for me, so I could only guess that Heidi told her all about my earlier phone call. I was sure she was just foaming at the mouth and waiting to pounce.

I wasn't disappointed. She grabbed me, almost yanking me off my feet, and hauled me into her apartment. She slammed the door behind me, brushed her hair out of her eyes and said, "Ok. Spill it."

"Spill what? Haven't you ever had sex before? You know how it works. You're a stripper, for Pete's sake."

She frowned at me. "You know what I mean. Where did you meet him? How did you get him to do it? What was he like?"

She was practically salivating, and I felt bad for her. Since she lost her job she had been trying to live vicariously through other people. The young, fresh stripper that replaced her was now headlining and the club hadn't called Kelly back to work. She tried other clubs, but there had been no takers. She missed the excitement of her job and she missed being drooled over by a slew of horny guys, although I'm not sure why. I decided to toy with her a little. There was no way I was spilling the actual details, but she didn't have to know that.

"Oh, Kell, it was the best night of my life. He was amazing." I sighed lavishly, pulling out all of the tricks I was taught in my high school drama club. Then I realized I wasn't lying after all. He was amazing. It was incredible. Damn it.

"Very funny, smartass," she said, disappointed. "I thought you'd share all the details from your incredible night with your best friend."

"Not a chance. You know I don't talk about that kind of stuff. Besides, why bother? It'll never happen again." I flopped down heavily on her crazily-patterned sofa. "I told him it was over this afternoon."

She picked up on that like a bloodhound picked up a scent. "This afternoon? What do you mean 'this afternoon?' Where did you go with him last night?"

Reluctantly I explained what happened. She listened with a rapturous look on her face. I swore that I'd help her find a job if it killed me. There was no way I'd disseminate every detail of my love life just to satisfy her craving for adventure. My life was not an open book.

When I finished my story, she said, "Do you think he's going to come back?"

"Why would he?" I answered. "I told him it was over."

"Yeah, but maybe he won't listen. Maybe he'll sweep you off of your feet."

"Not likely, Kell," I assured her. "My feet are firmly on the ground."

What I didn't count on is how hard he'd try.

Chapter 6

The one thing that annoyed me more than anything was to be woken from a sound sleep. I had been dreaming peacefully in my bed, my alarm clock not scheduled to go off for another hour, when my phone rang. I was ripped abruptly from a pleasant dream starring a dog, a bicycle, and some dancing circus clowns by the loud, shrill ring of my telephone. I groaned and pressed my pillow over my head and against my ears, and tried to block out the annoying ring.

Ugh. No use. I had to answer it or it would never go away. "Hello?" I barked into the receiver, irritated beyond belief.

"Hi, Caitlin. It's me, Ryan. I didn't wake you, did I?"

Ryan! What was he doing calling me? And how did he get my number? I decided to find out.

"Yes, you did. And how did you get my number?" I grumbled angrily into the phone. "I specifically remember telling you to get lost."

"I have a friend who works at the phone company," he said, and I could hear his sexy grin through the phone.

"So much for privacy, "I complained. "Why don't you lose my number? I mean it. I don't want this right now."

"I know, but someday you might change your mind. I'll be waiting." He gently hung up the phone.

I felt like throwing mine across the room. What a stubborn ass! Didn't I make myself clear?

Since I was up, I stormed to the bathroom and hopped in the shower. I had to get ready for work anyway, but now I was going to be able to enjoy some coffee and the paper before I got ready. Normally I got up a half an hour before I needed to leave, so this was actually a nice change of pace, although I was irritated at why I had woken up so early.

I enjoyed a leisurely pot of French Roast, the whole paper and a quick manicure before I left for work. I puzzled over why Ryan would have called me so early, and I had no answer. Weirdo, I thought. Just goes to show you that you shouldn't pick strangers up in the bar. You never know who you'll drag home.

I let myself out of my apartment and nearly tripped over a vase full of white tulips, a box of chocolates and a card. What the hell?

The card said, "Happy Valentine's Day!" and it was unsigned, but I knew who it was from. That explained the wake-up call. He wanted to make sure I was home to get my delivery. So now my stalker was not only annoying but he was also an early riser. Great, just great. I lugged my booty into the house, locked my door, and headed to work.

I work at a busy doctor's office downtown as a physical therapist to little kids who are recovering from accidents, surgeries or illnesses. My job is very tough but I love it. After clocking in, I helped Robbie Parker, whose right arm and hand were crushed in a car accident, try to print his ABCs again, and I held little Myrna Gray's hand as she tried walking on her prosthetic leg for the first time. It rubbed a little and she cried, but Myrna was a tough little cookie. Before long, she was actually taking some steps on her own.

As rewarding as all of that was, I was distracted. I kept thinking about Ryan and why he was pestering me when most guys would kill to have a one-night stand with no strings attached. Talk about a major role-reversal! What was with him? I actually got up the nerve to pull this outlandish stunt and I found a random guy to pull it off with. Things were not supposed to get complicated. But this was my luck. You'd think I'd be used to it by now.

Fortunately, the day passed quickly and I drove home deep in thought. I was amazed at Ryan's persistence and I wondered why he was so determined to force himself on me. Deep down I was a little flattered. After all, he was hot and he was after me. But, I was worried too. My last relationship, although it ended peacefully and diplomatically enough, still left me raw inside. I felt like a fool for even attempting to get close to someone else before my wounds healed. What was wrong with me? Even now I felt my resolve weakening again as I imagined Ryan's lips on my skin. I repeated to myself: 'I do NOT want a relationship right now.'

Once I reached my apartment, I headed toward my door and unlocked it. As I opened up, something that had apparently been wedged between the door and the frame fell to the ground. I bent over and retrieved it. It was an embossed envelope. Curious, I opened it. Inside was an engraved invitation to dinner at Les Deux on Saturday evening. Engraved? How the hell did he have time to do that? And how did he manage to get reservations? They were usually booked four months in advance, or at least that's what Michael always told me.

I couldn't believe the lengths this man was going to in order to force me into a relationship.

I decided to go to the dojo and work off some of my excess energy and irritation. Tsuyo-sa Dojo is a wonderful place, full of Asian art, bamboo plants and large studios where students learn martial arts. I had been coming here since I was a kid and I loved it. Before he died, my dad thought that every little girl needed to learn how to defend herself and he enrolled me almost as soon as I was out of diapers. My mom hated it, having been a ballerina herself, but she allowed it anyway, thinking that it would just be a matter of time before I swapped my gi for a tutu. Not a chance. This place felt like home and, through the years, I learned a lot under the tutelage of my sensei, Isamu Takeru. He was a gentle, wise man, straight from Okinawa. Usually, if I was upset or angry, I would come here and spar with him, and by the time I left my head would be clear. He had been a father figure to me ever since the day I found out my parents' plane went down over the Atlantic.

I changed into my gi and walked to the main studio. Isamu wasn't there but Bradley Shaw, a fellow student, was and he looked to be in the middle of a kata. Silently, I walked to his side and watched for a moment, then slid into the movements. We worked in perfect unison. This kata was one that Isamu had perfected and taught for years. The movements, while they required intense concentration and skill, were as familiar as breathing. It felt good to clear my mind and stretch my muscles. I lost myself in the exercise, concentrating only on the crispness of my forms, finishing them appropriately, and smoothly transitioning from step to step. By the time we were done, I felt better.

Bradley smiled at me and said, "Wanna spar?"

I grinned and we faced off, bowing shallowly to each other before assuming our stances. I dodged an open hand to the face and spun in time to miss a well-aimed kick to my sternum. I retaliated and landed a few light blows. We circled each other and sparred, each appreciating the skill of the other.

"What brings you here today, Catie? Normally you don't come in on weekdays." Bradley sidestepped to avoid a punch and smiled at me. "Something on your mind?"

"Yeah, but I can figure it out. Just needed to clear my head, you know?" I said, slightly breathless. Brad was quick and strong. Having trained together since we were kids, we were well-matched in skill, but he was giving me a run for my money today.

"Guy troubles or work troubles?"

"Guy. Michael left."

Brad stopped in mid-strike, falling out of his stance. "What? When?"

"A couple months ago. But it's getting a little better. It's really ok. I think. It's just, well—oh hell, Brad. I did something, and now I don't know what to do."

My normally straight shoulders slumped and I looked at Bradley in defeat. He had always been like a brother to me and a lot of times I felt more comfortable talking to him than I did with my girlfriends. I had always been able to more easily relate to guys.

He led me to the edge of the room and we stood together by the low teak benches that hugged the far wall. He slung a friendly arm around me and I rested my head on his shoulder. "So, spill it. What did you do? Something to Michael? Did you hit him? Good for you!"

I snorted. "No, but I seduced a stranger."

"You? You've got to be kidding me. Why would you do something like that?"

"Let's not go there, ok? I did it, and now I don't know what to do about it. He won't leave me alone."

"Have you looked in a mirror lately? I wouldn't either if you seduced me. I just don't see why you would pull a stunt like that. You could have been hurt."

Bradley pulled away from me and frowned in concern. I felt bad for even telling him. I was ashamed at what I had done already and his disapproval went straight to my heart. He was right.

"Well, if it's any consolation, he seems like a decent guy and he wants me to go to dinner with him on Saturday night. Kind of defeats the purpose of a one-night stand, huh?"

"Catie, you're better than that. Maybe you should go to dinner. Maybe he'll make an honest woman out of you."

"Very funny. Why do I need a relationship?"

"Well, why don't you?"

"I don't know. I just think that I need a break or something. Do you remember when my parents died?"

"Yeah, you had a rough time in class. You kept breaking form and crying. Sensei was worried that even karate couldn't settle you. But you snapped out of it eventually, right?"

"I don't know. I think that it's something that I'm still dealing with, on the inside. I felt so abandoned when my parents were killed. Like they didn't love me enough to stay alive, like it was my fault their plane crashed. I felt so guilty about it and, since Michael left, I've been feeling the same way. When am I going to stop feeling like a lost, lonely little kid? I just don't understand. Why do people keep leaving me?"

To my embarrassment, I was crying. I brushed a few tears from my cheeks and wrapped my arms around Bradley's midsection. He hugged me and said, "I don't think they're leaving you. They're just moving on. That's what you need to do. You just have to figure it out. But don't go doing anything stupid."

"I think I already did. And now I'm paying for it."

"Well, maybe you're right. A relationship probably isn't the best thing for you right now. Maybe you need to figure out how to stand on your own first. Sensei would probably say, 'Fall seven times, get up eight.' Just keep getting up, Catie."

He brushed my hair back from my face and wiped a wayward

tear from my cheek. I hugged him and said, "You know, if I hadn't been distracted, I would have kicked your ass today."

"In your dreams, Creampuff."

Chapter 7

After my workout I headed home in a much better frame of mind. I could get up again, couldn't I? I just had to get over it and trudge on. I was bound to find me somewhere. I'd call Les Deux and cancel the reservation that thickheaded suitor of mine made. Then I'd find another apartment or at least change my phone number. Amazing sex or not, he'd just have to get over me and take the hint.

I bounded up the stairs to my apartment and stopped short. A tall, dark, handsome, annoying man was standing by my door, leaning against the wall next to it. What the hell was Ryan doing here, again?

"So, did you get my invitation?" he asked me, grinning boyishly.

"Yes. I'm not interested. I'm lactose-intolerant."

"Well, we don't have to order dairy."

"I'm allergic to gluten."

"I'm sure they have gluten-free cuisine."

"I'm a vegetarian."

"Veggie platter it is."

"Can't you take a hint?" I glared at him. He didn't seem to mind.

"Can't you?" he smirked at me.

"Are you really that dense? I said I don't want this. I don't want you. Why won't you leave me alone?"

"Because I like you, I think, even though you haven't been that nice to me. Are you always this bitchy?" He grinned, and I felt my resolve weaken. He really was too cute for words.

"Yes, I'm always this bitchy. And I want to be alone."

"Why?" he asked seriously.

I didn't know.

"Just because. I really think you'd be better off if you went and found someone else." Ok, that excuse sucked, but it was all I could think of.

"Let me be the judge of that. I want to get to know you. I think you're sexy, funny and stubborn. I happen to find that a very attractive combination. Please say you'll come to dinner."

"We'll see. I don't like being badgered."

"Well, it's a good thing I'm a man and not a badger. See you Saturday."

With that, he grinned at me again and walked away with a bounce in his step that I found immensely appealing. Nonetheless, I rolled my eyes and let myself into my apartment, locking the door behind me. You never know who is going to show up and try to finagle an invite inside.

After much hemming and hawing, I finally decided to go to Les

Deux to see what else my resourceful stalker had up his sleeve. I would just have to tell him over their fabulous pâté and caviar that I was not going to start dating him, no matter what he came up with next. I called Ryan and accepted, sulkily. As I hung up, I thought I heard a whoop on the other end of the phone line.

The week passed quickly and, even though I didn't want to feel excited for the upcoming dinner, I was. Little gifts started appearing on my doorstep daily, like a beautiful blown-glass paperweight, a crystal rose, a box of doughnuts. I accepted each gift, albeit grudgingly, and wondered how I was going to get it through his head that we were not going to get into a relationship. I was scared, I could admit that. I just didn't want to admit that to him.

Saturday rolled around and I struggled with what to wear. The first time I met him I had an agenda, and I dressed to attract attention. This time, I wanted to deter my stubborn suitor but I had no idea how. I couldn't very well go into Les Deux looking like a slob. That was a fancy place. So I was stuck looking good, which grated on my nerves. Why hadn't I developed a face full of pimples over the course of the week? That would have been extremely helpful. But as I looked in the mirror on Saturday afternoon, I cursed my clear skin for the first time ever.

I found a siren red dress and paired it with a black lacy shawl, black pumps and a sparkly black-beaded choker. I piled my dark locks on top of my head and secured them with a band made of the same shiny beads. What I wouldn't have given to put on a pair of old jeans, a baseball jersey and a ball cap! I had always been a tomboy and I felt most comfortable in sporty clothes. I only dressed up when it suited my mood or when I was going out with my girls. I hated feeling forced to dress well. I applied makeup, pouted in the mirror because I had to apply makeup, and headed downtown.

Les Deux was always a favorite romantic getaway with Michael, and I felt weird going back there with another man. *This is not a date*, I thought, trying to convince myself. *This is a chance to tell that crazy fool that I won't be seeing him anymore. He can take his presents and his engraved dinner invitations and boyish charms and stick them you-know-where!*

Despite my resolve, the ambiance of Les Deux sucked me in. The crystal chandeliers sparkled, the candlelight cast romantic flickers around the dimly-lit room, and the linen on the tables was pressed meticulously and draped to perfection to the floor. Soft orchestral music was piped into the dining room and the air smelled of elegant fine cuisine. The maître d' was especially solicitous, greeting me by name as I entered.

"Your party is waiting, Ms. Edison," he murmured with a cultured

French accent, grasping my elbow and ushering me solicitously to Ryan's table

Ryan stood up to greet me, placing his cloth napkin on the table as he rose. He looked like sin, all long and lean in a navy suit with a navy and silver tie. His dark hair was styled to perfection and there was a twinkle in his eye that was hard to resist. I gulped once, turned to the maître d', thanked him as he pulled my chair out from the table so I could sit, and sank into the seat.

Ryan sat and said, "You look beautiful, Caitlin. How are you tonight?"

"I'm fine. Listen, this is nice but it's so unnecessary. You know how I feel. Why are you wasting all of this time and energy and money on something that isn't going to go anywhere?" I felt horrible for ruining such a carefully planned mood, but really, he needed to hear what I was trying to say. I didn't know how else to do it.

"Let's not worry about that tonight. Let's just enjoy each other's company, ok? Now, how about something lactose-, gluten- and meat-free?" he suggested, pouring some of the wine, opened to breathe, into my glass. I smirked at him and tried to relax. At least he had a sense of humor.

Sipping, I studied him. He certainly cleaned up well and he seemed to enjoy my company. So what was the worst that could happen?

I found out two hours later.

It must have been the wine, or the atmosphere, or those damn hormones again, because after our lovely dinner was over and he walked me to my car, he followed me to my place. Before I could open my car door to let myself out, he was there to open it for me. He didn't even wait for me to completely unfold myself from the driver's seat before he lifted me into his arms and kissed me breathless. He must have really had a thing for parking lots. This was exactly what happened the last time we were in one together.

What was going on? One minute I was sane, calm, poised, cool and collected, and the next minute I had my tongue in the mouth of a practical stranger who seemed intent on starting something I thought we had already finished. But he was so firm, so warm and rugged underneath my hands. I lost myself in the moment, in him, and even though I knew it was a mistake, I led him up to my apartment once again.

If the first time was good, the second was exponentially better. The hunger that I had been trying to repress burst to the surface, rendering me helpless against its force. He was my captor. I was his captive, and a willing one.

Though I thought I had some idea of what to expect, I was in no way prepared for the power of his lovemaking. He was an artful lover and his mouth trailed kisses over my body, teasing and tormenting me endlessly.

Breathless, I begged, and he acquiesced. Together we sought to put out the fires raging within.

It was a long time before we tired of each other. My last thought before falling into a deep sleep was that I'd have to start over from scratch now. I really had to convince him to leave me alone and let me have my one-night stand in peace.

The morning sunlight streaming through my bedroom window the next morning warmed my bare back, and I stretched luxuriously. I suddenly remembered that I was not alone and rolled over with a startled jump. He was lying on his side, facing me, propped up with his head on his hand.

He said, "Good morning," and stroked my hair with his free hand.

"Hi," I croaked. "Uh, listen...," I started, but he beat me to the punch.

"Yeah, I know. You don't want a relationship right now, blah, blah, blah. What I want to know is why" He looked at me sincerely, and a little angrily. I felt immediately worse. He had been nothing but nice to me, and I was being a shrew.

"Ok. You asked me once if I just moved in here, right?" The

words tumbled out in a rush. "Well, there used to be more furniture here because there used to be another person here. I had a boyfriend that fell out of love with me and I don't want to go through that again. I only wanted this hook-up, or whatever it is, because my irritating virgin friend said that it would make me feel powerful or some such nonsense. And of course, with my luck, I pick the one guy in the whole godforsaken town who isn't satisfied with a one-nighter."

His jaw dropped open and his eyebrow rose. He stared at me with a bemused expression on his face. He seemed torn between wanting to throttle me and wanting to pounce on me.

I took advantage of his silence and continued. "You wanted to know, now you know, so get off my back and out of my bed. And quit trying to weasel your way back into it because it's not going to happen, Mister!" I spat these last words at him, glaring at him with blood in my eye, daring him to cross me.

And oh, he did. He rolled suddenly, trapping me under his length, and his mouth stopped the tirade that was poised to come spewing forth. He shut me up all right, and left me with no doubt about how he felt about my rant. Our lovemaking was angry, staccato, and brilliant.

When we finished, he rolled off the bed, grabbed his clothes and headed to my bathroom. I lay there, stunned and confused, and thoroughly defeated. He emerged from my bathroom dressed in his dress shirt and slacks, his suit coat draped over the crook of his elbow. He paused by the side of the bed and looked at me with hard eyes. "Well, you wanted a one-night-stand, consider it done. I won't bother you again. My advice—don't start something you aren't prepared to finish."

With that, he stomped out of my bedroom and, after a few seconds, I heard my door shut with enough force to rattle the windows.

I lay in bed for a while, trembling. I never thought about what my scheme would do to the other person. Well, now I knew, and I didn't feel good about it. It sucked to be used.

I eventually regained my composure and got out of bed. After I showered, I headed to the kitchen. On the counter lay a business card. It read, "Officer Ryan Ashford, Pittston Police Department." His office and cell phone numbers were listed.

Well, at least I had good taste. He was a cop. He was one of the good guys. And I had just pissed him off.

Damn it. I liked him. I had to admit it. He had been nothing but nice to me, arranging a beautiful dinner, dropping off presents, and trying to woo me. And I hurt him. Well, the good news was that I had contact information for him now. I knew where I could find him. And if I killed Heidi for putting such a hare-brained idea in my head in the first place, he could arrest me. Even though I knew I'd never call him, I put his card in my wallet.

Operation One-Night Stand was a complete triumph. So why did I feel so awful?

The rest of the day passed uneventfully. I beat myself up a few times and cried a few self-pitying tears, but I snapped out of it. I put on my gi and ran myself through a particularly brutal kata to work out the frustration and angry energy that coursed through me. After my workout, I showered again and went downtown to try to find a new couch, and dining room table and chairs. I arranged delivery and swung by the Thai restaurant near my house to grab some khao man kai. I sat down in the kitchen to eat my lonely meal in silence. I wondered if this was what I was destined to do for the rest of my life. The emptiness was excruciating and, this time, completely self-imposed.

After a bottle of white wine and a good night's sleep, I felt better about things. I had done it. I accomplished what that stupid article suggested. Now all I had to do was sit back, enjoy myself, and make different choices now that I was a loose woman. Bring it on. Yeah, I was still lonely and I knew that I had some issues to work out, but maybe I was headed in the right direction.

I set out for work in a reasonably good frame of mind. I cranked the volume of my car stereo and shouted along to the trash rock I found, and I didn't notice the sirens or the flashing lights until I reached the front door of the doctor's office. Shit! What had I done? Had I been speeding?

A tall, dark, handsome cop exited his car, adjusted the brim of his cap, and walked to my car window. He tapped on the glass and I rolled it down.

"Excuse me, Miss. Do you know how fast you were going?"

No, I didn't.

"Uh, no, Officer. I'm sorry. I wasn't paying any att—Oh!" I looked up at my inquisitor and gasped. It was Ryan! I was safe! Or so I thought.

"Ryan, thank goodness it's you. Listen, I'm sorry about—"

"License and registration please, Miss." What the hell was this? Didn't he recognize me? Or was he taking my suggestion to heart? Oh, crap.

"Ryan, listen, I'm sorry about everything. I know that I'm a jerk and all, but you don't have to do this."

He held my gaze in a stony stare, no flash of recognition in his eyes whatsoever. I guessed he was a little mad. I fished my license and registration out of my glove box and handed them to him meekly. He turned on his heel and walked to his car, presumably to run my plates.

It seemed like it took forever and, meanwhile, Dr. Ross came to the front door of the doctor's office, staring out and frowning at me. I saw Megan and Sallie, the two nurses, peeking out the front windows, pointing and giggling. Great. My boss and the two biggest gossips in the office had just seen me get pulled over. I'd never live this down. Maybe I could threaten to karate-chop them.

After three eternities, Ryan came back to my car with my license, registration and a piece of paper. It was a ticket. A goddamned ticket!

"Miss, this is an appearance ticket for you for the charge of speeding. I clocked you going 47 in a 30- mile-per-hour zone. If you choose to plead guilty to the charge, mail in the fine of $130 by the date marked on the ticket. If you choose to plead not guilty, your appearance date is also listed on the ticket. Have a good day, Miss, and drive safely."

He strode back to his car, turned off his lights, and drove away, not even glancing back at me in his rearview mirror.

Oh, he was good.

I fumed the rest of the day. Megan and Sallie pretended to

console me, but they tittered about my traffic stop all day, heads bent together like they were connected. By the time lunch came around, I wanted to hide. I made it through my afternoon appointments, just barely, and stomped to my car.

What was that on my windshield?

An illegal parking ticket? For parking in a handicap parking space without the appropriate placard! What the hell was this all about? I wasn't in the ... *oh*. When I pulled into the parking lot and spied the flashing lights, I stopped where I was, which happened to be in a handicap parking space. And I was so embarrassed and irritated at Ryan for pulling me over that I hadn't noticed. The jerk could have told me, but no, he came back and issued another ticket. For another $200. This irritating man was costing me a fortune.

I drove home in a state of fury. I huffed and puffed and about blew my door in when I reached my apartment. I slammed the door shut and stomped inside, throwing the tickets on the kitchen counter. I briefly considered ripping them up, spitting on them and setting them on fire, but there was probably a law against that too. This was crazy. What the hell was he trying to prove?

The worst part was I didn't blame him. If I had been scorned the way I scorned him, I'd probably retaliate too. But jeez, $330 was a lot of money to cost someone else just because you were a little pissed.

I called Heidi and tried to holler at her for getting me in this predicament, but she was busy reading to a couple of blind kids so I had to cut my rant short.

Instead, I ran a piping hot shower, rolled my shoulders under the steaming spray to work out the kinks, and contemplated balancing my checkbook.

After all, I had fines to pay.

Chapter 8

Ryan's penchant for ticket-writing had gotten seriously out of control. By the end of the week, I had amassed four additional tickets for the strangest of things: parking too close to a fire hydrant (what fire hydrant?), unsafe backing (when I was pulling forward), violating odd-even parking restrictions (while I was parked in a parking lot) and driving the wrong way on a one-way street (also while I was parked in a parking lot). The tickets cost me an additional nine hundred dollars and my checkbook couldn't take much more of this nonsense.

Finally, I decided to confront the jerk and demand that he stop harassing me.

I drove to the precinct and parked very carefully. There was no way I was getting a ticket in front of the police station.

I walked into the main cop-area (what do they call it, *a bullpen?*) and was confronted by an older lady cop with dark, gray-streaked hair that was rolled into a bun at the nape of her neck, horn-rimmed glasses that tipped up at the corners and were held to her person by a chain, and a smell reminiscent of Kelly's Aunt Clara, a chain-smoking peppermint candy addict. She looked down at me from behind her horn-rims and said in a nasally, smoker-from-the-Bronx voice, "Can I help you?"

"Yes, I'd like to talk to Officer Ashford about these tickets, please."

She pointed to the chairs lined up against the wall opposite her counter and said, "Have a seat."

She picked up her phone and dialed. I sat and fidgeted. I always hate waiting.

It took about ten minutes after she explained who I was and what I was there for, but finally she said, "The officer will see you now. Follow that hallway to the end and take a left. His office is the third door on the right."

I stood up and jogged down the corridor. I had tickets to fight and I wasn't going to wait until I had my day in court.

Even though it was open, I knocked on his office door and waited to be acknowledged. He sat at his desk in his official uniform, looking pressed and polished and delicious. His lips were pursed in concentration and, as I unwittingly remembered the feel of them on my body, my mouth watered. Damn me and my stinking sexual needs anyway.

He glanced up, frowned, and motioned me inside the door.

"Close the door." It wasn't a request, it was a demand from someone used to being obeyed. It annoyed me but I followed his order.

"Listen, Officer—I don't know who you think you are, but you can't just go around issuing false tickets to people. I can't afford this horseshit!"

I threw the tickets on his desk and watched his face turn red. He stood up and his bulk filled the little room.

"Well, I can't afford to be played with, Miss." He stepped forward in a stance designed to intimidate and flung my insult back at me with force magnified times ten.

"I wasn't playing with you. I just thought that we could—I don't know—fool around with no strings attached. Damn that stupid magazine anyway."

I threw myself into the chair in front of his desk and looked at him belligerently. I expected him to grab his handcuffs and cuff me and, to my consternation, I realized that I probably would have enjoyed it.

"Did you just say 'magazine'?" He looked at me incredulously, a goofy smile starting to spread across his face. He sat back down and leaned backward, looking at me disbelievingly.

"No, I—never mind. It's nothing," I muttered. Me and my big mouth.

"So, you read something about this in a magazine?" He smiled again and started to chuckle.

"Yeah, so what? So Heidi told me about this stupid article about random hook-ups and how they're supposed to help women feel powerful when their life turns to shit and so I did it, but you weren't supposed to be there the next day. I blew that part. I guess we should have gone to a hotel or your place, but how was I supposed to know? It was my first time doing something like this, you know." I knew I was rambling but I couldn't stop myself. I really didn't want to have to tell him my reasons for doing what I did, but it looked like I had no choice.

"You know what? I think I read that article," he mused.

"Yeah, right," I muttered, scowling at him.

"No, seriously. But let's get back to what you were saying. Why has your life has turned to shit?"

That was the last thing I expected him to say, the last question I thought he'd ask. But ask it he did, and I had reached the point of no return a long time before.

"I was lonely. And horny. But mostly lonely. My breakup with Michael sucked. It was peaceful, and it was nice and friendly, but it still sucked. And this damn magazine said that I'd feel better and good things would happen if I randomly hooked up with someone. It was supposed to make me feel desirable and powerful again."

"And did it?" His question was earnest, and so were his eyes. The anger was long gone and in its place was compassion, something I hadn't expected.

"No, mostly I just thought of how unfulfilling one-night stands are." I caught the look on his face and quickly amended, "No, not that way. But emotionally. I wanted to be close to someone again. I couldn't distance myself like I thought I could. It was too nice. You were too nice. But I don't think I'm in the right place for a relationship right now, you know?"

"Yes, I know. You've said so before—a few times." He smiled and the corners of his eyes crinkled. I never noticed it before. It was really sexy. "Listen, I have an idea."

"What?" I was wary, but the pull between us was irresistible. I didn't know how much longer I could fight it.

"Why don't we just talk regularly, maybe have dinner once in a while, and see what happens, no pressure?"

Hmmm. No pressure. That sounded nice and pressure-free. I didn't know if I could do it, but at that moment, staring into those deep black eyes and that handsome face, I thought it might be worth trying. There was just one thing I had to do first.

"Well, ok, but how about those tickets?"

Chapter 9

All charges were dropped (he said he was planning on dropping them anyway—he just hadn't known how else to get my attention) and I agreed to meet Ryan for dinner the following week at Pizzazz, the pizza joint a few blocks from my office.

The whole week, while I waited for our upcoming date, I was nervous and easily distracted. Ryan called me a few times and we talked for ages. I found out that he was recently divorced and he had a son named Benjamin. Benjie was six, and apparently very smart for his age.

Ryan was upset that his marriage hadn't worked, but he had known for a while that the end was near. I felt for him. I had subconsciously known that my relationship with Michael had been destined for failure for a good length of time before it actually imploded. Even though I had known, it still stung.

I wondered why Ryan and his wife had split up. I had been too shy to ask him and I was trying not to become too involved. I guessed that it had something to do with his job. I'd heard that being a cop's wife was tough; you never knew when your husband wouldn't be coming home.

Even though I could tell that he was still bothered by his breakup, he said he didn't regret a thing. After all he had his son, and he wouldn't trade him for the world.

I didn't know how I felt about dating (yes, dating) a man with a child. I had never done that before and, even though I worked with children every day, I could hand them back to their parents and go home every night by myself. My stuff didn't get destroyed and I could watch what I wanted on TV and eat what I wanted for dinner. I was good with kids but this whole thing made me nervous. This tentative, no-pressure relationship was still very young, and even though we had come to know each other very intimately, there was still a lot we had to learn about each other. Dragging a kid into it seemed like rocking the boat, and I was still resisting the idea of getting into a relationship. I wasn't ready to give myself to someone who would probably just end up leaving me like Michael did, like my parents did. I knew I had to move on, but it was a slow process.

Still, I liked him, and I wanted to give it a shot. I wanted to try to get to know him and see what developed naturally. I needed to prove to myself that what happened in the past was in the past, and that I could move on and maintain a healthy relationship. This was the first step.

I dressed for our pizza date with care. I didn't want to appear too sexual or too frumpy. I decided on jeans, a cute plaid button-down top with a white cami underneath it, and my favorite sneakers. I pulled my hair into a ponytail and lightly applied makeup.

Pizzazz was busy but I spotted Ryan easily. His bulk took up most of one side of a booth in the far corner of the pizza parlor. He looked amazing in his form-fitting white t-shirt. The muscles in his arms were highlighted by his shirt sleeves and made me instantly feel warm and wanton. It appeared that his hair had been freshly cut and he was clean-shaven. His eyes picked me out as soon as I walked in the door and he stood up to greet me. I gulped as I noticed the way he filled out his faded jeans.

He gave me a friendly squeeze and a kiss on the cheek, and ushered me toward the booth. He smelled amazing. Lust flooded my belly like a warm bath. Why did the man have to be so damned appealing?

I was just about to accuse him of trying too hard to seduce me when I noticed the small head nestled against the booth-seat opposite of where I was standing. The head was attached to a young boy with short sandy curls and bright brown eyes. His olive complexion matched that of the man standing next to me who all but quivered with excitement.

"Benjie, my man, this is Caitlin. Caitlin, Benjie."

He smiled at his son, pride puffing up his chest until I thought his heart would explode through it. Benjie smiled at me and waved his chubby little hand. It appeared slightly grimy, as though he had been hard at play before his dad dragged him to dinner.

Well, this was the last thing I expected. It was going to be awkward enough to sit through dinner with Ryan for the first time since my confession, and he had to drag his little mop-top son into it? Luckily I had my karate training to make me strong in the face of danger—and little boys.

"Hiya, Benjie. How's it going?" I asked, just like I would any of my therapy patients.

He simply smiled at me and patted the bench seat next to him. I sat.

He cuddled himself against my side and said, "You're pretty. Daddy says you're nice too, and I have to be on my best behavior or there'll be hell to pay."

"Benjie!" Ryan gasped and I giggled. I could learn to like this kid.

We settled in to order pizza and, true to his word, Benjie was as good as gold. He and his dad obviously had a great relationship and their easy banter and carefree, loving antics had me in stitches. By the time our pizza arrived, I was smiling and having fun, albeit grudgingly. Maybe dating wasn't such a bad idea. However, I was still a little uncomfortable. It felt almost like Ryan was forcing me into something that I wasn't ready for, like we were playing "house."

Benjie got pizza sauce all over his shirt and howled like a banshee about it. Apparently, Iron Man shirts are hot commodities to six-year olds. I grabbed my napkin, dunked it into my glass of ice-water, and dabbed at the stain as best I could. My blotting tickled and made him giggle. Ryan looked at us with a thoughtful expression on his face.

I tended to Benjie, but deep inside, my insecurities were shouting at me to be careful. They insisted on knowing why was I here at this moment, pretending to be a family with a divorcé and his son? What good would come out of such a thing? Would I end up hurting not only a man but a little boy too?

And why was Ryan forcing this? He said there would be no pressure. The more I thought about it, the more I panicked. I stopped smiling and grew anxious. Soon, my long-standing psychosis reared its ugly head and I did the only thing I felt I could do—I tried to bolt.

"Excuse me, I have to get going," I said, abruptly swinging my legs out of the booth and getting to my feet. I grabbed my purse and dashed out of the pizzeria. I was running scared.

"Caitlin, wait!" Ryan must have seen the look of utter terror on my face because he jumped up, instructed Benjie to stay put for a minute, and ran after me. He reached me before I made it to my car and grabbed my arm to stop me.

"Where are you going? What's wrong?" He looked puzzled. I didn't blame him.

"I just have to go, ok?" I shrugged away from the grip he had on my arm and tried to get into my car.

"Will you stop? Boy, you are one confusing, frustrating woman!"

He grabbed my arm again and spun me to face him. His expression was somewhere between irritation and pleading. "Listen, Benjie's mom had an appointment that she couldn't get out of, so she asked me to take him. I wasn't about to say no because I don't get to see him very often as it is. And I didn't want to miss out on our dinner either. Sorry if I wanted things both ways, ok? What are you so afraid of?" He glared at me.

I knew what it was but I was dreading telling him. I was afraid of liking him more than I should and getting my heart broken, or breaking his heart. After all, it was just supposed to be a one-night stand.

Still, I was acting like a complete idiot. Of course he wasn't trying to play 'family'. He was just trying to have a nice dinner with his son and a new friend. I really needed to stop shying away from any sort of closeness or familiarity and jumping to silly conclusions. Yes, I was scared of being abandoned again, but maybe it was time to let go of the fear. I decided to take a leap.

"I'm sorry. I'm just so mixed up right now. Are you sure you want to get to know me? I'm really a mess." I peeked up at him apologetically. I really did feel like an ass now that my initial panic had faded.

"Yeah, I'm glutton for punishment. Besides, I thought we were going to split the tab. No dining and ditching." He put his arm around me and guided me back inside the restaurant.

Benjie looked up at me winningly. He smiled a cherubic smile and said, "Are you over your temper tantrum now?"

Chapter 10

I had to admit, after my little episode, I had fun with Ryan and Benjie. The kid was really cute and he seemed to like me. That did worry me, but I figured that this—whatever it was—wouldn't last anyway, so it wouldn't be an issue. He wouldn't have time to get too attached to me before his dad decided he'd had enough of my emotional roller-coaster.

My main problem was resisting Ryan's 'no-pressure' pressure. He met me for lunch at work every week, causing Megan and Sallie to whisper and titter like old ladies, dropped off dinner some nights, and called me regularly. It seemed like he was forgetting about his promise to let things develop naturally. The man was campaigning like a political candidate. But why? I told him that I didn't want anything serious. I was slightly worried about all of the time we spent together. As much as I was starting to enjoy Ryan and his attention, I was scared. Still, I tried to be game and get over myself, and one balmy Saturday we went fishing.

I hadn't held a fishing pole since before my parents died, so I was a little rusty. Because of my inexperience, Ryan decided to take me and Benjie to a little pond he knew. It was nestled like a jewel in the center of a forest crown and it was as serene as I imagined

Heaven would be. A light breeze made little shimmery ripples in the water and the sun threw dazzling sparkles onto its surface. It was delightful.

Benjie whooped and hollered as he raced toward the water, breaking the stillness. I glanced at Ryan and smiled. I had a feeling that this was going to be great. I imagined lazing in my chair with the sun on my face and the breeze in my hair, reveling in the peace and beauty of the scenery while fish nibbled on my hook. Why I imagined that, I don't know, because little boys and peaceful stillness go together like peanut butter and sardines.

From moment one Benjie was a handful. He was an exuberant little boy with a giant zest for life. He raced up and down the bank, knocking over our chairs, bumping our poles and squishing our bait. He hollered loud enough to wake the dead, not to mention the fish we were trying to catch. I doubt that there was a single fish that would be caught off-guard in the pond. He asked countless questions about fishing, the clouds, the trees, and why fish had scales when humans didn't. That was all in the first twenty minutes of our trip.

"Can we go swimming, Daddy?" Benjie peered up at his dad impishly.

"Not today, champ. The water is too cold."

"Aww. Is the water cold, Catie?" he asked me innocently.

"I don't know, Benjie. It looks pretty cold." I ruffled his hair and smiled at him. He was sweet, even if he was hyper.

He scampered off again and continued to trash our little setup. I had just righted my chair for the fourth time when I heard a squeal from behind me. I was perched close to the water to give Benjie ample room to run away from the pond, but I forgot the fact that little boys are clumsy. I heard another squeal and a "Whoa!" and felt a crash. Suddenly, we were flying through the air together toward the water. I braced myself, flung my arms around Benjie, and held my breath.

Splash! Yep, the water was cold. And little boys squirm a lot, especially when they accidentally end up in a pond. I hefted the gasping, wriggling, wet little mess in my arms and plodded out of the water, pants sopping and sagging, my long hair covering my face in soaked strands.

Ryan was there immediately, grabbing Benjie and hauling him out of my arms. He deposited his dripping son on the bank and held out a hand to me. I grasped it and climbed up on shore.

There I stood, water pouring out of my clothing, my hair a nasty wet tangle, my new shirt completely ruined. The look on my face must have been one of utter and complete resignation.

Ryan inspected Benjie, gave him an affectionate squeeze and turned to stare into my eyes. He smirked, and I returned his cheeky grin. The grins turned into smiles, the smiles into snickers, and the snickers into outright laughter. We guffawed in unison. Of course, I hadn't thought to bring a towel and neither had Ryan. But Benjie didn't seem to mind being wet. He only ran faster, allowing the breeze he made to dry him.

And before we left, he lifted his little face up to gaze at his dad and said, "Before we go, can me and Catie go swimming again?"

Before I knew it, a very pleasant month had passed. I saw both Ryan and Benjie regularly and I began to get accustomed to them both. I still kept my distance, and Ryan tried hard to bridge it, but we had reached a comfortable stalemate. He seemed content to let things develop as they were, and I tried to come to grips with the fact that there was a man in my life. He didn't sleep over often, and I preferred that. I wanted my solitude. I felt like I needed it to work things out.

I meditated for hours at a time, trying to make peace with my past and my present. It was an uphill battle and, deep down, I still missed Michael. His absence was a little death inside me. He had been my friend as well as my lover, and not hearing from him was tough. I almost resented Ryan for trying to force something that came so easily with me and Michael. It wasn't Ryan's fault but I knew I would need time to sort through things before I gave myself completely to him.

None of my friends or family had met my new beau yet, and I preferred to keep it that way. I felt like he was my dirty little secret, and things were still so fragile between us that I didn't dare complicate things further.

Even though I think he would have preferred things otherwise, Ryan respected my wishes and kept our dates private, meeting at restaurants across town or at my apartment. We went on long walks and took Benjie fishing and bowling regularly. But I couldn't hide our relationship forever and, the more I was with him, the more I wondered why I would want to.

Ryan invited me to a policeman's picnic in mid-August and I reluctantly agreed. Well, I begged and pleaded not to go, but he insisted that I had to. I'd been seeing him, more or less, for the past four months. I had been quite unsuccessful in resisting him. However, I was still concerned about making our relationship official. I was also worried about meeting all of his coworkers. What would they think? Had he told them about his (my) conquest? How would they treat me? As a lady or a whore?

The night before the picnic, I tossed and turned and woke up a few times in the middle of the night bathed in cold sweats. Ugh. Since when had I become such a date-o-phobe? I had been making such great progress lately, too. I guessed that the main thing that worried me was that I didn't know if I felt better because of my budding relationship with Ryan or in spite of it. That bothered me. A lot. Was I destined to be one of those women who defined themselves by the men they were coupled with? Would I lose my identity and become just half of a whole? I was so confused.

The other thing that bothered me was that Ryan was a great guy. I knew it was a silly thing to be bothered by, but I was. Yes, he had a terrific job. He was a great dad. He was gorgeous. I truly liked him. But I felt that something was missing. Not with him—with me. I had to find that before I would be willing to dive into something that would last.

Until then, he'd just have to deal with my neurotic mood-swings and erratic behavior. Poor guy. I had really tested his patience thus far. Still thinking, I drifted back into an uneasy sleep.

The morning of the picnic came much too quickly. I hadn't slept much at all and the dark circles under my eyes weren't flattering. The sun was already up and blasting humid heat down upon the town, so wearing any sort of makeup that would surely melt off my face was out of the question. I settled for ice cubes, cucumbers and a quick facial instead.

I dressed with care in a lightweight pink cotton dress and sandals. I wanted to look my best. There was no sense in embarrassing Ryan, relationship insecurities or not. He expected me to be there as his date, and I wouldn't humiliate him in front of his friends.

He came to pick me up at 10:00. Thanks to some strong coffee, the cobwebs were just about cleared from my brain by then. He knocked on the door and smiled widely when I answered it.

"You look amazing. Are you ready?"

He kissed my cheek swiftly and backed up. He was learning not to get too clingy and close. He knew I was still the slightest bit gun-shy, although I hadn't told him all of the reasons why. He just assumed I was still dealing with my break-up from Michael. Whenever we discussed our past, I skipped over any mention of my family.

"I'm ready." I smiled back. Insecurities or not, I was going to make this a good day for him.

We drove to Brandt Park and pulled into a parking lot already packed with cop cars of both the on- and off duty variety. He got out first and opened my door so I could slide out of his Toyota. I heard a deep male voice shout, "About time you got here, Ashford!"

Ryan laughed, put his arm around my waist and led me toward the crowd gathered around a large barbecue in which a pig turned on a spit.

"That's Danny Gleason. He's my partner." He pointed to the broad-shouldered guy with the crew-cut slowly turning the pig. We walked to the barbecue and a chorus of male voices welcomed us.

"Hey, Ashford! What took you so long?"

"Who's the lady, Ashford, and what the hell is she doing with you?"

"Aren't you going to introduce us to your friend, Ashford?"

"Is she single?"

"Hey, Ashford, who's your date?"

I blushed. There was nothing like a gathering of males to bring out the testosterone. Still, these guys were cops. How bad could they be?

I found out over lunch. Cops were raunchy. The jokes that flew around the picnic table would have mortified sailors. But the guys were great, and it wasn't long before they and their wives sucked me into their easy camaraderie.

"Hey, Ashford, why don't you bring Caitlin over to the ball field so you can show her how real men play baseball?" one young officer shouted. "Then she can teach you later!"

"You're on, Waterman." Ryan chuckled good-naturedly. He grabbed my hand and led me to the ball field.

There were perhaps forty people on the field, either settling in to watch or warming up to play. Ryan took his place among the players and I scooted into the bleachers next to Danny's wife and Waterman's girlfriend. We cheered and clapped when our men came up to bat. They were all pretty athletic, given the nature of their jobs, and they were obviously close-knit. For a minute I imagined that I was really part of the group too. It surprised me how good—how right—it felt. Was this what I had been depriving myself of? The idea of opening myself up to new people suddenly didn't seem so terrible. We cheered as the men came up to bat and the guys took tongue-in-cheek jabs at each other. I felt myself relaxing and before too long I was actually enjoying myself.

Right after the fourth inning, an unexpected visitor showed up on the field. Her hair was honey-gold and curly, hanging just below her shoulders in lustrous waves. Her eyes were green and coolly observant, taking in all of her surroundings in a carefully disdainful way. Her outfit screamed uptown, completely out of place in such a relaxed atmosphere. I wondered briefly if she was brass from the precinct but decided that she looked way too sophisticated for police work.

After me, Ryan was the first to notice her. He straightened and approached her.

"Nancy, what are you doing here?" He spoke quietly, but he kicked the dirt in front of him with his sneaker viciously, spraying Nancy's hose with gravel and showing his temper in a rare display. It was unusual for Ryan to be anything but laidback.

She glanced down with disdain and shifted her weight. "Just dropping off some paperwork. Have this back to my attorney's office no later than Monday."

"I'll have it back after my lawyer looks it over. Don't push me, Nancy."

"It would take a bulldozer to push you, you stubborn ox."

"You know, I've been very nice about this whole thing so far. I'll thank you to be civil about it and, while you're at it, quit filling Benjie's head with nonsense. You know how many times he's asked me when he's moving to New York?"

"So? He's inquisitive. And we are moving. There's nothing you can do to stop me—us."

"Watch me. You can't take my son. You aren't allowed to leave the state with him if I forbid it. And I forbid it."

Nancy scowled and flicked a speck of invisible dirt off her cool green suit jacket. "I'd like to see you try, you bastard. You can't stop me. Not anymore."

I got to my feet and wandered over to where they were standing, just to be a presence. I knew that Ryan could take care of himself but I also knew there was strength in numbers. Maybe the snooty woman would take the hint that she wasn't welcome if a few more people stared her down. I silently stood behind Ryan and studied her. She was pretty but there was something ice-cold in her eyes, her very demeanor, that was off-putting.

Danny came over to stand next to Ryan and raised his voice in a mocking taunt. "Hey, Nancy, slumming again, huh?"

"It looks that way. Get off my case, Danny."

"Not a chance, *Mrs. Ashford*. Not until you get off Ryan's."

"Oh, Ryan hasn't seen anything yet. Wait until he gets a load of what type of lawyer real money can buy."

"Get the hell out of here, you bitch. I'll get you for trespassing," Danny growled, stepping forward menacingly.

Ryan flung his arm out and caught Danny in the solar-plexus to hold him back. "That's enough, Danny. Nancy, I'll talk to you later. As you can see, I'm busy."

"We'll talk later, alright—with our lawyers. Good-bye, Danny. So nice to see you again."

"Bitch!" Danny sneered.

She turned on her ice-pick heel and strode off the field on long, tanned legs. The icy silence left behind chilled me to the bone.

Ryan walked over to me with a look of disgust on his face. "Let's go."

I raced back to the bleachers to grab my pocketbook and murmured a quick goodbye to the women. I had to run to catch up with Ryan. He was almost to the parking lot before I did.

"Wait up, would you?" I huffed. He merely held the door of his car open and ushered me inside.

Jaw clenched, he got in, buckled, and pulled out of the parking lot with a little more speed than I thought was necessary.

"So, I take it that was your ex-wife?" I asked, trying to break the silence.

"Yeah." He was rigid in the driver's seat, staring straight ahead with desperate focus.

"Does she always show up for the policemen's picnic?"

"She used to. This year was a surprise."

"Well, at least you were the only guy who brought two dates. That has to count for something." I smirked at him, trying to lighten the mood.

He chuckled. "I didn't think of it that way." His face lost its brief animation once more and he frowned.

"Do you want to talk about it?" I asked.

"Do you want to hear about it?" he returned.

The funny part was, I did. I nodded and he looked at me speculatively before pulling off the road.

We parked in a vacant lot and Ryan sat straight in the driver's seat, a distant expression on his face.

"Nancy and I met twelve years ago. We were no more than kids. I thought she was great. She had drive, ambition, and great legs. I thought she was the one, you know?"

I nodded and waited for him to go on.

"She and I got married eleven years ago and, at first, things were great. But her parents had money and they didn't want Nancy stuck with a cop for a husband. They wanted her to marry some other guy, this young, snazzy stockbroker they had hand-picked. For a long time she resisted. We had Benjie and things were good. But money was tight with the baby, and Nancy got scared. She ran to Mommy and Daddy and they offered her a small fortune. But there was a catch. She had to ditch me and go with the stockbroker. And, you know what? She did. After all we had been through, she tossed me over—for money." He stopped and swallowed. The look on his face was one of pure agony.

It was sad and the pain he was feeling was familiar. I knew all about abandonment, about hurt. I reached over and stroked his arm, just to let him know I was there for him.

"Well, our marriage ended last year. And you know what? As soon as the ink dried on our divorce papers, she married that asshole. And, of course, with her daddy's money she got custody of Benjie, she and that scumbag stockbroker who couldn't give two shits about my son—my son! Now they want to move to New York City for some job the dickhead got. Last week I filed papers in court to prevent her from taking him away from me. I guess she's a little pissed."

I took his hand and rubbed it. I could understand his anger, loss and sadness. It was obvious that he was struggling with all three. I felt twenty times worse than I did before for giving him such mixed signals. He could obviously use someone to care for him right now. Spooked or not, I was going to be that person.

"And you know what? She takes my money every week. She always said how my paycheck wasn't enough to live off of in a third-world country and she takes my money every single week without a word. I'd give her double to care for Benjie, but it grates on me that she takes it when she was so embarrassed by it before. What the hell is wrong with me or my money?" He lowered his head to the steering wheel and rested it there. I stroked his back silently, not sure of what he wanted me to do or say.

He laughed once, a harsh, mirthless laugh that showed his pain. "What a woman."

I slid over in the seat until I leaned up against him. I rested my head on his shoulder and continued to rub his back. After a minute, he turned toward me and said, "Thanks."

He said no more, but I knew what he meant.

Chapter 11

After the picnic, my relationship with Ryan changed. He had opened up to me and it was my turn to step up and help him through his ordeal. It was a load of responsibility, but I didn't mind. In truth, it wasn't a hardship; he was a great guy. I felt sorry for Nancy. She had no idea what she had given up.

We started spending more time than ever together, and it was my turn to reassure him. One of the most frequent topics of conversation was Nancy and her new scumbag stockbroker husband.

"I'll kill him if he takes my son away. How the hell can he even think about moving away and taking Benjie away from me? I'm his father, God damn it, and I have joint custody."

I tried to reassure him. "No judge in his right mind will take Benjie away from you. You have to calm down and do what the lawyer said. Document everything and let them know just how she is when you have your day in court. This anger won't help. If you threaten him, he'll have fuel against you."

"I know. But he's my son. My life. I can't be without him."

No matter how hard I tried, I couldn't calm him down. I was just as worried as he was that Nancy and her slimy husband would succeed in taking Benjie away. It would crush Ryan. That little boy was everything to him; it would kill him if he couldn't see him regularly. It was hard enough for Ryan to give him back to his mom whenever their time was over. I couldn't even imagine how he would feel if there was a distance that large between them. Ryan's lawyer assured him that he would have a fighting chance at his case, but we were both still worried.

I was also worried that Nancy would use my relationship with her ex-husband to somehow wrest Benjie away from his dad. Ever since Nancy saw me at the picnic, she seemed to zero in on our relationship and do everything in her power to turn Benjie against me. What she didn't count on was Benjie's firm devotion to his dad and his genuine fondness for me. She tried to fill Benjie's head with all kinds of lies, and we heard it all.

"Daddy, what's a prostitute? Mom says that Catie's a prostitute."

"Daddy, what did Catie steal? Mommy says Catie is a thief."

"Daddy, Catie shouldn't lie. Mommy says Catie lies and that people who lie go to Hell. I don't want Catie to go to Hell."

"Daddy, when I move to New York City, Mom says you and Catie won't come visit me. I'll miss you. Why won't you come visit me?"

Ryan held his son and reassured him, but his eyes were hard and dangerous as they met mine. I hated seeing Ryan so upset but I had no comfort to offer him. All I could do was be there for him and try to understand what he was going through. It was painful to watch and I felt myself sliding down into the depression he was suffering.

To distract Ryan, I threw a dinner party one night at my apartment. I invited Kelly and Heidi and their current men. Ryan could make a mean steak and potato dinner, so I asked him to cook while I busied myself cleaning and redecorating. We gathered around my new dinette set and toasted each other over red wine.

Kelly brought an obnoxious twenty-something named Camden. He was preppy from the top of his gelled-up head to the soles of his Bass loafers. His Dockers were neatly pressed and his button-down was so starched he made noise when he moved. I didn't like him. He was a pantywaist with soft, well-manicured hands and a store-bought tan. He even had a phony New England accent (I think he was trying to mimic a Kennedy). Where Kelly found him, I had no idea, but I planned on telling her to drop him back off there.

Heidi also surprised us with her choice of a date but for a different reason. Peter was a solid middle-class hottie with a killer smile and eyes only for her. He had a decent bod and a great sense of humor. He was smitten, it was easy to tell. He blended with us as easily as scotch blends with water. Before too long we were all laughing at Peter's jokes, except for Camden, of course. He tried to one-up Peter and didn't seem to notice when his jokes fell flatter than pancakes.

Kelly and Heidi were in rare form, drinking wine and flirting. It was refreshing to see them in action, cooing in the ears of their beaux, wrapping themselves around them, throwing innuendos like rice at weddings. And both girls seemed hell-bent on embarrassing me and my new man.

"Hey, Catie, did you ask Ryan to break out the handcuffs yet?"

"Maybe he'll let you see his billyclub."

"Catie, you've been a bad, bad girl. You need arresting."

"Maybe he'll lock you up and punish you for your crimes…."

I giggled uncontrollably at the antics of my friends. There was something so fun and alive with all of us together that it was hard not to smile. I felt freer than I had in a long time. It was a welcome change from the intense relationship that Ryan and I had suddenly developed. I'd been trying so hard to be there for Ryan that I had forgotten how to have fun. Tonight, I let it all go.

Ryan took it all in and watched me speculatively. A few times during dinner, I caught him staring at me with a brooding look on his face. When I looked at him, he glanced away quickly, embarrassed to have been caught studying me. I wondered what had him so curious. I never got a chance to ask him, though, because after dinner we moved into the living room and played cards. After a few more bottles of wine, my girls were quite tipsy and had obviously had enough, so their dates scooped them up and herded them out the door. They left blowing me kisses and giggling.

Finally, everyone left and it was just me and Ryan. He came up behind me as I was clearing the dinner dishes and wrapped his arms around me. He nuzzled my neck and said, "Well, that was… enlightening."

"What do you mean 'enlightening'?" I frowned, even as his mouth against my neck did fun, ticklish things to my insides. He had a mouth that would make a puritan tingle. But his choice of words irritated me.

"I thought that you might have been stiff and serious all the time. Now I see it's just with me."

I whirled around in his arms and said, "What exactly do you mean by that?"

"Normally, I'll talk to you and you'll just clam up. You don't smile, you don't laugh. You just sit there like a bump on a log and listen. When you're with your friends, you come alive. You actually have a great laugh, a beautiful smile. Why don't you let me see them? What are you afraid of?"

"For starters, being attacked for being who I am. If you recall, you're the one who pushed this relationship, Ryan, not me. I told you what I wanted, and you forced the issue. And I didn't think that you needed that frivolity right now. You have a lot going on."

"Who told you that you had to be all serious? This is my deal, not yours. I'll handle it and you're not doing me any favors by sulking with me. Not only that, you've always been that way. Why don't you lighten up and have fun every once in a while—with me? And besides, you didn't tell me what you wanted until after you had your way with me. That's pretty low and you know it."

"Damn it, it wasn't supposed to be low. It was supposed to be a one-night stand with a random stranger. You were never supposed to stay. What kind of guy does that?"

"A forever kind of guy. Caitlin, I don't know if you are aware of this or not, but I think I'm falling in love with you. But you've done everything in your power to push me away and leave me hanging. I don't appreciate being used, not even by the woman I think I love."

"Well, who asked you to love me? I told you before that I don't want a relationship."

"Then what do you want?"

I didn't know. I had been so caught up in what I *didn't* want that I had no idea what I really did want. I still didn't know. I liked him, sure, but what did that mean for the future? Was there a future with him? I had no idea. All I knew is that he was sexy as hell, standing there with his deep black eyes blazing, his face intense and his jaw taut. His stance was masculine and erect, and his hands were clenched into fists at his sides.

Suddenly, I had an idea of what it was that I wanted, although I wasn't sure it was quite what he was thinking. Still, it was worth a shot. There really was nothing hotter than an angry, fired-up man. And this one turned on my sexy side from the first night I met him. Damned if my anger hadn't completely turned into lust.

"I'll tell you what I want. You naked, in my bed, right now."

I moved toward him sensuously, swinging my hips and tossing my hair back behind my head. He read my mood and met me in the middle of the room, his hands reaching for me as mine reached for him. He grabbed my waist and roughly yanked me toward him, his mouth searching urgently for mine. My hands went wild on his back and his fisted in my hair, moving my head in concert with a deep, smoky kiss. Our clothing flew off and draped itself about my living room.

I moaned and backed up toward my bedroom. He was with me and we hit my mattress in a mad tangle of already-naked arms and legs. Our bodies joined urgently and I showed him what I wanted. Even if it wasn't what he had in mind, he was willing to work with me this one time.

He trailed his hands down my back, over my buttocks, stopping there to grasp me and pull me to him. He hauled me up on top of him and I stretched, moaning as I felt his heat warm my limbs.

I lowered my head to his and took possession of his mouth. Our kiss was smoldering. My hands frantically stroked over his muscles and sinew, racing over his chest, his shoulders, his midsection. I went lower and he shuddered. His hands gripped my waist and he drove us home.

I couldn't get enough of his body, his smell, his touch. He touched me. It was more than casual sex, and I knew it, perhaps for the first time. He was inside me, in all the ways that counted, and I couldn't get my fill of him. He was everything.

When we were sated, I propped myself up on my side and traced my finger over his chest. It was slick with sweat and I relished the dampness and the reason it got there.

I knew it was time to open up to Ryan the way he opened up to me. But I was afraid of what he would say. In truth, I was afraid of what I would end up saying. This was not something that came easily to me. But, I had to try, so he knew what he was getting into.

"Ryan, you asked me what I wanted. You asked me why I was so tight-lipped and, well, tight in general."

"Yeah, I seem to remember I did. Right before you ravished me."

"Sorry about that."

"I'm not. And besides, tight is good for some things." He smiled at me then, that sexy smile that did those tingly things to my insides. But, I would not get distracted.

"You know, there are reasons I am how I am. Are you going to listen to them or what?" I squirmed away from his mouth on my breast. I wanted to get this out while I still dared.

"Go ahead. Be my guest," he murmured, his breath warm and gentle now on my neck.

I pulled away from him and sat up. I took a deep breath and started.

"You know how you've never met my family?"

He nodded.

"Well, my parents were great when I was little. We were so happy, just the three of us. We had a great life. We were the picture-perfect family. When I was ten, they decided to go away for a week on a second honeymoon to Europe. Mom was a French teacher and she had always wanted to see Paris. So Dad bought a vacation package to surprise her and they left me with my grandmother for the week."

I paused when my voice started quivering and took a deep

breath. I had to get through this without breaking down. My heart was weeping, but I would not allow the tears to break through.

"We got word five hours after they dropped me off that their plane had gone down. There were no survivors."

Even after all this years, those words still echoed in my mind. *No survivors.*

Hard as I tried to control them, the tears broke through anyway. I wiped them from my cheeks impatiently. I could still remember that day vividly, and how I had clutched my Gran's hand so tightly when she told me that I bruised her. I had sat in my room for the rest of the day, staring out the window, willing them to appear in the driveway. Night had fallen and still they didn't come home. They were never coming home. I remembered my Gran's sobs echoing through the house, and the people who came over to sit and stare at me with damp, mournful eyes.

The day my parents' plane had gone down, a piece of me had died with them, and reliving it now was killing me all over again. I sniffed and continued, my voice breaking with every other word.

"I think when your security is rocked like that when you're little, it messes with you. I became very clingy with everyone I knew who showed me even the slightest hint of love or affection. When you've had that love and affection and it goes away, you want it back. I needed it. I felt so abandoned and I missed them so much. My Gran was not a loving woman. It's not like I was neglected or anything. It's just—well, let's just say that she made my teenage years difficult. She was never there for me and, no matter what I did, she disapproved. It was tough, to say the least. I think she must have blamed me for their death, and blamed them for dying and saddling her with me."

He frowned and nodded. I think he could see similarities between me and Benjie, and it pained me afresh. He probably was worried about Benjie feeling abandoned and unloved, and I was worried that my insecurities would open his eyes to what may happen to his own son if he lost custody. I vowed silently to give both Ryan and Benjie a lot of love and attention so they never had to feel like I had.

"Michael was always my friend. He lived across the street from me and our parents were close. When he found out that my parents died, he came over and sat with me for hours, just listening to me cry. I used to wish his parents would take me in so I could be with him all the time. One day, after a particularly vicious fight with Gran, he helped me run away. Of course, they found me a few hours later, but the point was he was there and he understood. He made me feel safe again. And in high school, he was the first guy who paid any sort of attention to me. I liked it. It felt nice being cared for and loved again. I never wanted that feeling to end. He was actually my first—and only—until you."

I shifted until I was facing him and then I took his hand. I looked into his eyes earnestly, hoping he saw what I wanted him to see in mine.

"After so many years with Michael, I was secure and then, all of a sudden, he ended it. He said that we had grown up but we never grew together. I loved our relationship but it really reached the end a long time before he ended it. I clung to him because I was afraid of being alone again. He was safe and he was secure, but he wasn't for me."

I sighed and wiped my eyes with the tissue Ryan handed me.

"I'm so afraid of the same thing happening again. And I'm afraid of liking you more than I should and getting my heart broken again. Inside, I'm still that scared, needy little girl who wants to cling. But I don't want to cling to the wrong person. I can't take another trauma in my life. I can't put myself into a relationship that has no future. I can't take the chance of giving my heart to someone else just to have them leave me the way everyone else has. I can't do it."

Ryan squeezed my hand and sat up. He faced me and looked into my eyes.

"Aw, Catie, it's about damn time you told me that. You think I don't see how haunted you are every time you look at me? I know about loss and trust, believe me. But let me tell you something. You said that when the plane went down, there were no survivors? Well, you were the survivor. You made it. Now it's time for you to move on. Can you try to give us a shot? I can't promise the outcome, but I can promise that I will never intentionally hurt you. I'll never use you and I'll always let you know what I'm thinking. Ok?"

He rubbed my shoulders and drew me into his arms, soothing me. I let go and sobbed. I cried for the little girl I was and for the woman I had become. I wasn't sure what this would bring, and I was still scared as hell, but I thought that it might be worth a shot. He would have to be patient, and if I was a little neurotic, so be it. He'd just have to get used to the whole package.

Chapter 12

Even though I unloaded on Ryan, and I really felt much better about things, I was still scared. I had finally accepted the fact that I was in a relationship but that didn't mean it would be easy to let go of my earlier insecurities.

Monday, after a particularly stimulating phone call from Ryan, I panicked at the thought that our relationship was based on sex. Freaking out, I called Kelly. "What if he really doesn't like me? What if he's just using me for sex?"

"Oh, my God, Catie. Chill out. If he was just using you for sex, he'd have run when you went all weird on him the first time."

"But what if he just can't figure out how to end it? I've already spilled more than I should. I've shared my innermost thoughts and feelings with him. I've never done that before and—"

"Get over yourself. It's not about sex. Listen, Camden is here, and he is all about sex, so I have to go." She hung up.

I wasn't satisfied, so I called Heidi. "Is my relationship with Ryan based on sex?"

"Of course it is, honey, but in a good way. Listen, the ladies' sewing circle is here and we're making quilts for the troops overseas. Can I call you later?" She hung up.

I wasn't satisfied but I decided to follow Kelly's advice and get over myself. Still, it took another round of phone calls to Kelly, Heidi and Ryan to convince me that we connected on several levels instead of one.

Tuesday, I worried that I would get tired of Ryan and dump him, hurting him and thrusting him into a shame spiral that he'd need therapy and several months of alcohol to climb out of.

"Well, are you planning on dumping him anytime soon?" Kelly asked me.

"No."

"Ok, then, so quit worrying about it."

I called Ryan. "Will you survive if I dump you?"

"Are you trying to tell me something?" he asked, amused.

"No, I was just wondering."

"I'm not sure. Let's not find out, just in case, ok?"

I hung up on him.

It took a lot of ice-cream and several more phone calls to Kelly, Heidi and Ryan to convince me that I actually liked Ryan and wanted something long-term with him.

Wednesday, I got scared that Ryan would get tired of me and dump me, pushing me back into the lonely oblivion that had threatened to all but swallow me whole.

"Catie, I'll let you know if I get tired of you, ok? I haven't run yet even though you're obviously crazy, so I don't think I will. Relax, would you?"

It took a shopping spree with Kelly and Heidi to make me realize that I was a strong, beautiful woman (with brand-new lingerie), and that Ryan would be a fool to get rid of me.

Thursday, I suffered a near-panic attack because I was actually in a relationship with a great guy who seemed to like me in spite of my flaws. What if I screwed this up? Would anyone else even bother to look twice at me, Miss Damaged Goods herself? It took a nap, a bottle of wine and a paper bag to get me back into the right frame of mind.

Friday, in spite of my week of growth, which I was very proud of, something happened that shook me to my core.

Michael called.

It started out as a normal day. I got up, shook out the cobwebs, and padded to the shower. I ran the water as hot as I could get it without scalding myself, and stood under the steamy spray, pushing my tumbled hair out of my face and allowing the water to pummel me awake.

I soaped, scrubbed, exfoliated and rubbed myself dry. I smoothed lotion into my invigorated skin and stood in front of my closet trying to figure out what I was going to wear. I had just narrowed my selection down to a khaki skirt, pink cotton button-down and cute strappy sandals or a navy wrap-dress with sexy heels when the phone rang.

I frowned. Who would be risking life and limb by calling me at this hour?

I exited my bedroom and ran toward the kitchen, trying to grab the phone before my voicemail got it.

"Hello?" I answered breathlessly.

"Catie? It's me. How are you?"

Michael! A voice that I never thought I'd hear again. Over the past few months, with the advent of Ryan in my life, I had forgotten how much I missed it.

"Well, hi. What are you doing?"

I was puzzled, and unwillingly pulled back into nostalgia. How many times had I heard that voice, deep and mild, on the other end of the phone line? How many times had I listened to that voice in bed next to me at night, murmuring sweet nothings to me, moaning in ecstasy?

"I, uh—thought we'd get together today, maybe for lunch? Spinell's?" His voice was now slightly uncertain as if he knew how much he was asking.

"Um, ok. I go to lunch at noon. Do you want to meet there, then?" I asked, frowning a little. What was this all about?

"Sure. I'll see you then. Catie, I'm looking forward to seeing you."

I hung up the phone without saying goodbye. I slid down the wall and sat with my back against it, feet splayed out in front of me like useless spokes.

I was having lunch with Michael.

My morning was wasted on me. The sun shone brightly on my commute; I barely noticed. The radio station I listened to religiously every day suddenly seemed to be playing all of my favorite songs; it could have been opera for all I cared. My little patients were making remarkable progress; I nodded and smiled, but the import was lost on me.

I was having lunch with Michael.

The time seemed to alternate between super slow-speed and hyper-speed. The office gossips, Sallie and Megan, stared at me and twittered together behind their charts.

"Distracted today, Catie?"

"Any more speeding tickets lately?"

Their blatant prattling barely registered. I kept glancing at the clock and it seemed at times that the minute hand barely moved and, at other times, it had wings.

Ryan called and asked what I was doing for lunch. I brushed him off, using work as an excuse not to see him. I felt guilty as hell afterward, but what could I do?

It was time for lunch with Michael.

The drive to Spinell's was quick. I arrived at only five minutes after noon. Still, Michael's F150 was already snugged into a spot on the side street by the restaurant.

My heart started pounding in my chest. It had been six months since I'd heard from him. Seeing him would be surreal, I was sure. I was also sure that I would need a lot more than another week of growth to bring me back to where I was before I picked up the damn phone this morning. I was truly taking a giant step backwards.

Spinell's had a cheerful atmosphere and killer manicotti. The warm yellow walls beckoned happily and the smell inside the restaurant made one's stomach growl instantly. Still, I wasn't hungry. My nerves were too raw. I was actually having lunch with Michael.

My eyes picked him out immediately. He was seated in a small cozy booth in the rear corner of the restaurant. He faced the door and he stood as I approached.

He had weathered the last six months well. His blond hair was freshly cut and styled, and he wore blue, the color I always thought made his eyes sparkle. He looked as though he had been working out; his chest seemed broader than I remembered.

"Catie! You look wonderful. Come on, sit! I ordered you an espresso. Is that ok?"

"Fine, thanks. You look great too. How have you been?"

I was truly curious. I knew how I felt without him. I wondered if he had the same feeling of being adrift in the middle of the ocean on a small wooden raft without a paddle.

"Just great." He smiled at me and I smiled back. It was hard not to. As curious as I was about why he called me, I was glad to see him. I knew that I still needed him, still missed him and still loved him, even though it wasn't in quite the same way as it was before.

In the past, my love for Michael had bordered on obsession. I needed him to help me feel safe, to feel secure, to feel wanted. When he left me, I lost my security blanket. I felt cold, lost and very vulnerable.

He must have known how I felt because his face softened and he said, "How have you been really, Catie?"

I gulped and felt tears well up in my eyes.

"Honey, I'm so sorry I left the way I did. But I had to."

I nodded, unable to speak.

He looked at me soberly and continued. "What we had was great, in its way, but it wasn't what either of us needed. I felt like I had to take care of you and, honestly, I wanted a girlfriend, not a child. And you needed to grow up, to come into your own. You needed a father, not a lover."

'That's not fair. I loved you for you, not because I was substituting you," I retorted.

"Catie, face it. You were a lost little girl and I was getting a little tired of waiting for you to grow up."

I wanted to protest again but realized he was right. Michael had been my crutch since we were kids and I could imagine how tiring it must have been for him to prop me up all the time.

At that moment, the waitress came with our drinks. She plunked them down and took our lunch orders. I steeled myself and looked up at Michael's handsome face.

"Michael, I'm sorry. I never knew you felt that way. I wish I had known. I would have tried to change things."

"No, you wouldn't. I don't think you could have. You had to learn to live without me at some point and it seemed like a logical time to start. Listen, enough of that. I have some news."

"What? News?"

"I'm getting married. Charlotte and I met about a year ago and we started dating soon after you and I broke up. She accepted last night. We're getting married in three months."

"Wow, that's ... great. Really. I'm happy for you."

I looked at him earnestly. I wanted to feel happy for him but really I was feeling abandoned all over again.

He studied my face intently, looking for the slightest bit of anger or sadness. I twisted my face into a suitably happy expression. I must have fooled him because he nodded slightly and sat back in the booth, relaxing. He became animated as he told me about Charlotte, her job as an engineer, the perks and the neighborhood into which they were thinking about moving as long as he could break his lease. It was hard not to toss my scalding espresso into his face.

After lunch he hugged me and kissed my cheek. I returned the hug, holding on slightly longer than was necessary. I missed him. Yes, I had Ryan, but Michael was an old friend, a relic from my former life and, even though I knew I had to let go, it was excruciatingly difficult.

He walked me to my car, hugged me again and promised to call me soon. I sat in my car and watched him take long strides to his truck. He got in and started the engine. As he pulled away, I put my head on the steering wheel and sobbed.

My former life drove off and left me, once again, in the dust.

Chapter 13

I couldn't bear to go back to work. My face was tear-streaked and I had developed a massive headache. The office gossips would have a field day with my unruly appearance, and I didn't trust myself to be supportive and gentle with my patients; I felt anything but.

I drove home instead. Once inside, the emptiness of my apartment was keenly apparent again. Why did I still feel the loss so sharply? It hurt, more than I thought it could.

I went straight to my bedroom and climbed in bed, fully dressed. I assumed the fetal position, wrapping myself around my pillow. I hugged it to my chest, my arms aching from holding on so tight. I wondered briefly if my mind was substituting the pillow for Michael.

I knew it was over, truly I did. And I knew that he had moved on. I thought I had. But it was obvious to me that I had a lot of healing left to do. Was it fair to hold onto Ryan while I did?

I didn't know. All I knew is that the pain returned full-force and it knocked me senseless. I also knew that I was currently in no condition to give my heart to Ryan.

We had made plans to meet for dinner tonight. I didn't feel like going anywhere or doing anything. I curled deeper around the pillow, sighing as a lone tear made another track down my cheek.

The salty drop found its way to the corner of my mouth and my tongue reached out to gather it.

I sighed quietly. I had to have some time to think. I closed my eyes and pictured Michael's face as it was then, and as it was now. I imagined his arms around me and inhaled deeply as I thought about his warm clean scent surrounding me.

I must have drifted off, because when I opened my eyes again, it was dusk. I was late for dinner.

I heard a noise from outside of my bedroom door and, moments later, little footsteps walked closer and closer to my side of the bed.

A warm, slightly clammy little hand patted my cheek, and a small voice said, "Catie, are you awake? You missed dinner!"

I rolled over, blinking my eyes to clear sandman's leavings, and held out my hand toward the voice.

"Benjie? What time is it?" I caressed his downy head and pulled him toward me. I nuzzled his neck and he giggled.

"What are you doing in here in the dark, Catie? Daddy was worried about you."

"Where is your daddy, Benjie?" I struggled into a sitting position, squinted and glanced around.

"Right here. Benjie, why don't you go and raid Catie's fridge? We'll be right out." Benjie scampered off and left me alone with

Ryan.

"What's wrong? Don't you feel well? I was worried."

He came to the bed and sat down next to me. He reached for me and wrapped his arm around my shoulder. With his free hand, he felt my forehead.

"I'm fine. I just need to be alone right now, ok? I'm sorry about dinner. I'll make it up to you sometime, alright?"

I tried to turn away from him but he pulled me closer and grabbed my chin in his warm palm. Gently, but with steel in his grip, he turned my face back toward his.

"What is going on?"

"I just need to think, ok? I saw Michael today and I just need to think."

"You saw Michael? Where? When? What the hell happened? Is that why you blew me off earlier?"

"He called. We met for lunch. It was just lunch. He's getting married." I burrowed my face into his shirt and started crying.

Ryan held me silently for a few minutes. Then he gently pried me off his chest and said, "Ok. You're going to be ok. Why don't you grab some things and stay with me for the night?"

"I can't. Don't you understand? I don't need to be babied. I just need to be alone. I'm an adult. I can handle things. You don't need to take care of me. I don't need a father, ok?" I said this fiercely. My conversation with Michael affected me deeply.

"What are you talking about? I'm not trying to baby you, for God's sake. I'm just trying to help you. Why won't you let me help you?"

"I don't need help. I can't rely on you. I can't rely on anyone but me. So just go away. Take Benjie to dinner and let me be by myself."

"You're one big, emotional, neurotic mess, you know that?"

"Yes, I know. But I want to be a big, emotional, neurotic mess by myself." I glared at him.

He glared back, trying to stare me down. I sat up straighter, deepened my frown, and scowled so hard I worried my face would freeze that way.

"Don't do this to yourself. Please."

"Just go. I want to be alone," I shouted at him. Why didn't he take the hint? I had to do this on my own, damn it.

He studied me for a moment and then backed up off the bed and toward the door.

"Fine. I'll go, but this isn't over. You hear me? I'll be back and we are going to talk about this."

He stormed out of the bedroom and I heard him yell for Benjie to get his fingers out of the peanut butter and get his butt in gear.

123

The door slammed. I was alone.

I was really alone.

Michael was gone. Ryan was gone. I was alone, again, and I had brought it on myself.

In my heart I knew that it was time for a change. Blaming my current relationship woes on my parents and Michael was getting old. It wasn't their fault.

Things happen. People fall out of love. People get married. People die.

Did I have to fall to pieces with every little exit in my life? I had to stand up for myself. I had to grow up and find my own way. I could not continue to base my worth on a relationship or lack thereof.

This was going to be the hardest thing that I ever did. But it was as necessary as breathing. I had to get my life in order before I dragged anyone else into it.

I lay back down in bed and closed my eyes. I'd work on me in the morning. I was exhausted.

Chapter 14

The morning after my meeting with Michael and subsequent blow-up with Ryan, I woke up feeling scared. Today was the first day of the rest of my adult life. What a frightening concept that was. When you hold onto ghosts long enough, they become part of you. Would I be able to let them go, to heal?

I'd soon find out. I had to exorcize the demons and learn to lean on me, and only me. My insides still ached, but I sat for a while in a meditative pose and willed myself to clear my mind. A random thought popped into my head. It was a Japanese proverb that Isamu liked to say to his students: *we learn little from victory, much from defeat.*

It occurred to me that I had been defeated. I had been tossed aside like yesterday's newspaper. I could let it eat at me or I could learn from it. I stood up with new resolve. Time to clean my proverbial house and learn from defeat.

My first project was to go through my old photo albums and purge every picture I could find of Michael. It took two hours and gallons of tears staining my face. A lifetime of friendship and love were documented in eight thick albums and it seemed like every page contained at least one shot of me and Michael. I relegated each of them to a shoebox. I couldn't quite bring myself to throw them away but I could put them where I couldn't easily grab them. I had to accept that it was behind me, that he was behind me. I was learning.

After that chore, I sorted through each room in my apartment, placing every gift that Michael ever bought me, every possible thing that could be tied to him, in a large heap. I bagged it and placed it by the door. Too bad the fire alarm was hard-wired into the fire station. I would have enjoyed torching every last thing. Instead, I'd go to the Salvation Army later and donate it all.

My apartment looked much emptier by the time I was done. With that chore finished, I decided to go whole-hog and do something that I never had the courage to do before.

Some things had occurred to me while I was purging. I found a lot of pictures of my family before the crash but very few from after. In the ones I found, Gran and I were always apart, and I don't think she had a smile on her face in any of them. Come to think of it, neither did I. I had some suspicions about Gran and the way she had treated me after I came to live with her, and I figured that while I was cleaning house, so to speak, I should really get down and dirty. It was time to face the rest of my past.

My Gran answered the phone on the third ring. She sounded

breathless, like she had run across the room to grab the telephone before her answering machine picked up.

"Hello?" Her voice was slightly cold, slightly uptown and slightly unwelcoming. But she was my Gran and I needed to know some things.

"Gran, it's me. How have you been?"

"Oh, Catie. Just fine. How are you? Still working at that doctor's office downtown?"

"Yes, for three years now, Gran."

Well, that's fine. What brings you to call today?"

"Gran, do you love me?"

There was silence on the other end of the phone line. This was not something that I had ever dared to ask my sophisticated aloof grandmother.

Finally she spoke. "Excuse me? Why in God's name would you ask me that question?"

"Nothing I do ever makes you happy and I just want to know why," I said softly. Then I surprised myself by adding a question that seemed to have come out of nowhere. "Was it because of Mom and Dad?"

"What? Don't be ridiculous."

"I don't think I am."

"Caitlin, what's wrong with you?"

"Nothing. I just need to know."

She sighed heavily. "I guess I can take some time today. Why don't you come over? We can talk."

I agreed and drove uptown.

Gran's house was stately, big and sterile. It had the appearance of a *Better Homes and Gardens* spread, and it always felt cold and foreboding to me. Gran had money and she used it to create a masterpiece of real estate. It could have been a posh museum. There was no real comfortable place to sit and rest, no place to put your feet up, no place that felt like it should be used. Driving up to the house, I felt the urge to turn around and go back, but the answers to the questions I had beckoned. It was time to learn the truth.

Gran answered the door dressed in a power suit. Her hair was freshly coiffed and her nails were meticulously manicured. My grandmother was a lady from the soles of her dainty feet to the top of her slightly graying, perfectly styled head, and I had always mortified her with my athleticism and tomboyish ways.

She looked down her aquiline nose at me ever so slightly, taking in my rumpled shirt and faded jeans. She did not approve, but what else was new?

She led me into the sitting room and sat me down on a plush, firm, very uncomfortable loveseat. She sat adjacent to me in a coordinating wing chair. She picked up a paper-thin china cup of tea from the pie crust table next to her and delicately sipped, pinky properly out.

"So, what brings this up now?" she asked imperiously. I always felt mildly like I should curtsey before addressing her.

"I just saw Michael. He's getting married to some other woman. That's all, really."

I knew she wouldn't approve of my hook-up with Ryan or my subsequent neuroses, so I was going to avoid telling her about him until I absolutely couldn't any longer. As much as she liked Michael, she always frowned upon my 'shacking-up' with him, and always said that I should be married before I lived with a man. What would she say if I told her I picked up my current boyfriend in a bar? I shuddered. I couldn't even imagine that scene, given her revulsion for all of my choices. Had I been a doctor, she would have been a holistic treatment advocate. Had I been Catholic, she would have been a devout Muslim.

"Well, that's too bad. He was a nice boy."

"Yes, he was. Is. But that's not really what I wanted to talk about. I wanted to talk to you about our relationship while I was growing up."

"Oh, good God. What does it matter? It's long over now. Why rehash the past?"

One of the main things that bothered me about my grandmother was her inability to look backward. I was a thinker, always had been. But Gran plowed ahead with a fuck-the-past attitude and moved on. I sometimes wished I could be like that and, other times, I was appalled by her insensitivity. Now was one of those times.

"Gran, I'm asking. Don't you think I deserve to know? What happened to my parents didn't just affect you, you know. It affected me too. Deeply. I think I deserve to know your motivations for hating me so much."

"Motivations? What motivations? Really, Caitlin, you make me sound so devious and evil. It was one of those things, that's all. And I don't hate you."

"Seriously, that's the best you can come up with? 'One of those things?' Who are you trying to fool?"

"I tried to raise you to be a good child, a good woman, but you didn't cooperate with me. You were a willful child and you never did do what I wanted you to."

"Gran, I was just a kid. I was little when you got custody of me. Don't you think your expectations were maybe a little too high?"

"I didn't want to raise another child. I had already raised my daughter and I wanted time alone. Then you came here and I had to give up my freedom to raise a child who wasn't my own."

"So you didn't want to share your precious freedom with a little kid who just lost her parents?"

Seriously, how low was that?

She frowned and her face grew red. "And maybe I resented your father for taking your mother on that stupid vacation. It's his fault she died. He took my daughter away and he killed her. There, I've said it. Are you happy now?"

Whatever I had been expecting, it wasn't that. I was stunned. I couldn't believe my Gran was that selfish. Or maybe I could.

"You know what you're saying, right? You're actually blaming my dad for the mechanical failure that brought the plane down. Since when did Dad pilot planes or perform airline maintenance?"

"You know what I mean. If he hadn't bought that silly, indulgent trip, she'd still be alive. Instead, she went gallivanting off with him and got herself killed just because she wanted to see the other side of the world to get time away from you."

I felt as though I had been slapped. "Gran, you don't know that. People die. Maybe it was just their time. But blaming my dad, and blaming me, isn't fair."

"Well, it wasn't fair for them to go away and leave me with you. I already raised my child. Why didn't anyone think about me?"

"So you would have preferred that I went into foster care? Your own granddaughter?"

"Yes. I would have."

"Oh, that's just great, Gran. Very nice of you. And generous. Who thinks that way about their only surviving relative?" I huffed in consternation. What a shrew she was sometimes.

"Catie, I have something to tell you." Gran's voice was uncharacteristically small.

"What is it?" Now what? The look on her face was unsettling. She suddenly looked old and afraid. I never remembered my Gran being afraid.

"You aren't my family. You were adopted. Shelly couldn't have kids. She was sterile, so they adopted you. Then she and that boy she married went and got themselves killed. They left me with a child they weren't meant to have. You're no family to me. That was their deal, not mine."

And there it was. The reason for my Gran's disdain. I had just been told the most shocking thing in my life. I was not my parent's natural child. I had been given up, and subsequently adopted, only to be abandoned again later. Was that where my fear of abandonment had come from? I had no idea what to think. This was huge. However, I didn't react emotionally, even though the situation called for it. I just wasn't sure what to do next, or how I should feel. Should I be upset, numb, shocked, hurt or even glad?

Instead, I surprised myself by coming across coolly logical and inquisitive.

"So you hate me because I'm not really your family?" I asked her.

"I don't hate you really. But I can't love you, either. I'm sorry if I wasn't good enough to you when you were little. I just couldn't stand it. I didn't want you. I already paid my dues. Don't you see?"

So that was it. End of story. It all made sense now—all the distance, all the disapproval, all the barely-suppressed anger. My Gran couldn't get close to me because she was too selfish to open her heart to a little girl who had no one else. It was absolutely unreal. I needed to leave. The emotions that I had thus far suppressed were starting to seep through and I didn't trust myself not to start screaming at her. I got up and headed for the door. I had a lot of thinking to do.

"Thanks for telling me. I have to go now, ok?" I opened the door and started out.

"Catie, wait. Why are you leaving now? Don't you want to discuss Michael?"

"No, I really don't. I think I have things figured out. Sorry to have bothered you," I called over my shoulder as I bolted out the door.

I escaped; there was really no other word for it. I ran to my car and got in, chest heaving, breathing unsteady. I thought back to what I had just heard and felt a jolt of shock rush through my body. My grandmother was too wrapped up in her own grief to consider the feelings of her only granddaughter, blood kin or not. And everything she told me rang true. She was selfish, always had been. She always considered her own needs first even over the needs of a ten-year-old child who obviously had some emotional issues to work out. Truly amazing. The worst part was she saw nothing wrong with her behavior.

And what a bombshell she dropped! I was adopted? Holy shit.

But it all made sense in a weird kind of way. No wonder the old bat didn't like me. I wasn't hers. Try as she might, she never could control me and mold me into someone I wasn't. That must have burned her biscuits but good.

Driving home, I recounted what she said and marveled at her coldness. And I was angry that I allowed myself to be tangled and twisted inside because of her. Well, no more. It would end now. I was sick and tired of being a victim. I would no longer allow my excuse-for-a-grandmother's mistakes to screw up what I was sure was the first healthy relationship I ever had.

I thought long and hard about my real parents. I wondered why they gave me up and why my adoptive parents chose me. *Adoptive parents.* That was going to take some time to get used to. Maybe even a whole lifetime. My parents, the wonderful people I remembered and missed every day, were not really mine. The shock turned to anger, but I tried to turn it into curiosity instead so it didn't eat me alive. Did they have a choice, my adoptive parents, or was I the first available baby on the market? I almost wished that I had been randomly given to them, the first available baby matched with the next people on the list, like a heart being given to a donor. I think it would have hurt even worse if they had chosen me, then left me so suddenly. I felt utterly alone. I had no one, no family to speak of. I was a castaway on a deserted island. Hell, I was the island, lonely and unapproachable.

And my real parents—were they alive? Did they ever think about me? Did they know that the people who took me off their hands had died? And would it make a difference? After all, they got rid of me once. What would stop them from getting rid of me again? It stung, this rejection that I had been unaware of. Maybe that was why it hurt. When you know the people who don't like you, you can rationalize. This was different somehow, this blind dislike, almost like they didn't give me a chance to fit in with their lives. If they had, maybe they would have liked me, if only...

There were so many 'if onlys' and I pondered them constantly. Still, after a month of tossing around these latest revelations in my head, I felt like I was in a better place. I considered that my birth parents may have been in a bad way when they had me. Maybe this was the best chance they felt they could give me. Maybe they gave me up with love in their hearts. I could live with that. And maybe someday, when I had love in my heart, and forgiveness, I could find them and see if we could start over. I dreamed about it at night, and sometimes I awoke smiling.

And one day I knew what I had to do.

Ryan. I had upset him. I had to make amends. I just hoped he'd forgive me and that it wasn't too late.

Chapter 15

The day I went to Ryan, I paced and worried for a good hour before I got up the courage to drive to his house. I was scared of being rejected. After all, my own grandmother rejected me; how could I guarantee that someone who had known me for a lot less time would welcome me back? But I missed Ryan and I felt so bad for hurting him. I had to apologize and let him know how much I had grown.

I also realized something else during my time of reflection. I had family after all. Kelly and Heidi were my sisters, Bradley Shaw my brother. Isamu, my father figure since my parents' plane went down, was family. It occurred to me that even though there weren't any blood ties, they were mine and they were always there for me. It was enough. It more than made up for Gran's cold distance and it also showed me that blood wasn't the only tie that bound.

After making peace with my past, at last I was ready to think of my future. I drove to Ryan's apartment and knocked on his door. There was so much I wanted to tell him.

He answered warily, his eyes hurt and confused even after all this time. "What is it, Catie?"

"Can I come in?"

He nodded and moved aside, allowing me access into a living room that could only be described as upscale-bachelor. Long black leather sofas hugged the walls that were painted brick red. A gigantic flat-screen TV and surround-sound system dominated one whole wall, and trendy urban paintings were hung on the rest. Splashes of yellow, green and blue from the art kept the space from feeling too overwhelming, and a colorful geometric design rug softened the meticulously restored hardwood floor. Ryan was neat, so everything was in its place except for a pizza box that was currently askew atop the glossy black lacquer coffee table.

"How are you?" he asked me, concern peeking through his anger.

"I'm ok. I really am. And I'm sorry."

"For what? Seeing Michael? For standing me up on our date? For not calling or seeing me in over a month? Benjie was worried about you." That was a low blow, but I ignored it.

"No, I'm sorry for being such an ass all these months. I've come to some conclusions that I thought you should hear."

"Oh? Well, by all means enlighten me." His voice was hard and I could tell he was trying to hurt me the way I hurt him.

"Can we at least sit?" I gestured to his sofa. He rolled his eyes but sat. I parked myself next to him, looking into his eyes earnestly.

"Ryan, I'm sorry. I know I've said that already. But I mean it. I've been such a fool, but I found some things out recently and I'm done living in the past."

"What things? What happened with Michael?" He was wary again and my heart ached. I knew what he must have thought when I told him I had seen my ex.

"Michael is getting married next month to a woman that I think he must have started dating before we broke up. He didn't say so in so many words but he did say that he met her a year ago, and we were still together then." And why else would he have made it a point to mention that they started dating after we broke up? The bastard. I pieced this together over the past few weeks, and realizing he may have cheated on me was enough to get me over him. I was better than that and I deserved much more.

"So, after he dropped that bombshell, I sort of fell to pieces. I've missed him and it didn't hit me how much until I saw him in the restaurant. He said that he was tired of taking care of me, that he wanted a woman, not a child. That's why I said what I did to you. I don't want you to have to take care of me. I want to do it myself. And I know you don't want me to take care of you. You just want us to be ourselves, but together. I get that now."

His frown eased a little and he took my hand. I squeezed it and continued.

"But that's not the biggest thing. I saw my Gran. She told me that she resented me my whole life because I wasn't her family. I was adopted. She never forgave my mom or my dad for dying and saddling her with me. So she emotionally abandoned me and holed herself up with her grief. Now I'm free."

"I'm glad for you, but what are you saying? Are you abandoning me?"

"No. Don't you see? I think you do love me and I think I love you. For the right reasons. I'm not going to let her mistakes ruin what we have. We do have something. I think it's time to let go of the past and give the future a shot. Ryan, I think I finally grew up. And I want to keep growing, with you."

He grabbed me fiercely and hugged me to him. His lips brushed my hair, my temple, my ear, my cheek. His mouth found mine and he kissed me urgently. He stood, lifted me in to his arms and carried me into his bedroom. He undressed me carefully, whispering to me all the while.

"Don't worry me like that again, ok? I thought you were getting back together with Michael and it scared me senseless. I can't bear to lose you."

"You don't have to. Thank you for being patient with me."

I moaned a little as his hands wandered tenderly over my body.

He knew where to touch me to drive me wild and he used his considerable skill to show me the depth of his feelings now.

"Even though you're crazy, I still do love you. Just do me a favor—warn me the next time you have a meltdown, ok? Don't put me through that again."

He bent his head and kissed me deeply. We tangled together on the bed and, for the first time, we made love. It was the sweetest thing I ever felt. Tears of joy ran down my face as we coupled, and I knew that the anguish I had gone through was worth it.

Later, we snuggled on his sofa, still naked. His warm hand brushed down my back toward my rump and we lay together, simply enjoying being with each other.

"So what now? Do we move in together?" he asked quietly.

"Not yet. I'm not ready to do that yet. Let's get used to this. I've done a remarkable job of getting over things but I'd rather not push it, ok?"

"Actually, it is. I understand. Truth be told, I'm not sure it's a good idea anyway with Nancy fighting me about Benjie. We have court soon and I'm not going to give her any fuel to use against me."

I nodded. I knew he was worried about the upcoming custody hearing. If she decided to move, who would be able to stop her? Would she kidnap the boy, make up some nonsense about Ryan to convince the judge to side with her? And poor Benjie. He must be so confused. This whole thing was tough on him, and Ryan was worried about how Benjie would handle things once the court proceedings were underway.

Ryan shifted and sat up. He looked pensive.

"Catie, can I ask you something?"

"Sure, anything." I was concerned. Ryan was obviously upset, even with our newly-rekindled relationship bliss.

"How do you think Benjie will handle it if I lose? Do you think he'll be ok?"

"I think so. He's a resilient kid. He seems like he's handling things fine and I know he doesn't believe all of the stuff that Nancy says. You know that."

"Yeah, but I worry. I know how messed up you were when your parents died and I can see changes in Benjie. He doesn't laugh like he used to. He hugs me so hard when he leaves and he seems so sad all the time."

"Ryan, it's going to be ok. Don't let my neurosis affect how you see Benjie. These are two completely separate circumstances, ok?"

He seemed satisfied for the moment and held me close again.

"How about lunch?" he said, shooting me a grin. "I was just about to eat when you came in here and threw yourself at me."

"Threw myself? You wish. But yes, I'd like some lunch. Can I ask one more favor?"

"Of course." He looked at me curiously.

"Can we go eat with my sensei? I want to put the last of the past behind me and I want you with me. I think it's time you got to meet the non-crazy members of my family. Strike that—I want you to meet my real family."

"Sure, but can we get dressed first? I don't want to meet him naked."

I giggled and got up, pulling him up with me. It took a while to get dressed, because once we hit his bedroom, he pinned me and kissed me breathless, which of course led to another enthusiastic round of sex. By the time we were done with each other, it wasn't lunch time anymore.

We called my sensei and arranged to meet him at his house for dinner.

Isamu lived on a shady street in the suburbs. Large homes set far back into deep front yards were the norm here and Isamu's was no exception. When he came here from Japan, he bought this house. Since his children were grown and still in Japan, and his wife had died years earlier, he rambled around in this excess of square footage, eventually surrounding himself with three rambunctious chocolate Labs that he affectionately called Eenie, Meenie, and Miney. They were gentle giants and they kept Isamu company. I loved them.

Isamu pushed past the large wagging tails and happy, drooling grins to let us in. All four occupants of the house looked elated to see us and I took great pride in introducing Ryan to my surrogate family.

I had told Isamu about Michael a few months before, but I never mentioned a new man. Still, he took it in stride and, instead of feeling left out, he welcomed Ryan cordially. Isamu was always happiest when he knew I was happy. I had looked forward to this night. I knew Isamu would make it a true homecoming.

We were shepherded into the kitchen where a pot of spaghetti was fragrantly warming on the stovetop. A loaf of fresh Italian bread graced the kitchen table and Isamu had set out three place settings. For a pure-blooded Japanese man, he could cook some wonderful Italian food. Three dog bowls were lined up on the floor and three hungry Labs drooled in anticipation. Isamu always cooked enough to feed everyone and tonight was no exception.

We all sat, Isamu dished up and we got into the serious business of eating. With Isamu, it was eat first, talk later. All three dogs cleared their bowls quickly and lay on the floor in a furry heap, resting and occasionally belching.

After our meal, we pushed back from the table and sat sprawled in our chairs, lounging. I knew that we were finally ready to get down to some serious discussion.

"So, Caitlin, what brings you here tonight?"

"Well, I wanted to introduce you to Ryan and I wanted to talk to you."

"Yes? That is nice. It is always wonderful when you come by. And I am honored to meet your friend. What do you for a living, Ryan?"

"I'm a police officer, sir. With Pittston PD."

"Oh, a police officer. Well, I will not have to worry about my Caitlin, then, will I?"

"Sensei, you don't have to worry about me. You've taught me karate practically ever since I could walk. You taught me how to defend myself, remember?"

"Of course I remember, but I still worry. So, Daughter, what did you want to talk about?"

"Sensei, I went to see Gran."

"Yes? And how is Grandmother doing?"

"The same. But she told me some things about my childhood."

"We should go into the living room. We will be more comfortable there. Ryan, would you like a beer?"

Ryan nodded and Sensei shuffled to the fridge. He withdrew a frosty Bud and handed it to Ryan. We walked to the kitchen and settled down on the couch.

"Caitlin, that was a long time ago but I can understand why you must talk about it. Anytime a relationship ends, it brings up questions about other relationships."

I nodded. Isamu had always been very perceptive.

"Sensei, Gran told me she didn't want me."

Isamu frowned. The rejection I suffered hurt him as badly as though he were the rejected. "Sometimes people hug their grief and their sadness to themselves like a blanket. They learn to live with its weight and they do not know how to live without it. I think that Grandmother lives with a great weight and I do not think that she can lift it off of her shoulders, so she takes it out on you. She will not allow herself to be free. One must be free of hatred before one can feel love."

"I think you're right."

"But it is time for you to relieve yourself of your burden. You must start a new chapter in your life. If you let your loss swallow you, you will turn into Grandmother. To let love into your heart, you must give up the hate. You have much to heal for."

"Oh, Isamu," I hugged him and sniffed a little. "I love you."

"Isamu loves you, too. Now, who wants dessert?"

We left his house two hours later. I felt like I was where I needed to be; finally, I was free. I held Ryan's hand as he drove us back to his place. I hoped that he felt as good as I did but something told me that I was alone in my contentment.

I knew that he was thinking about what my sensei said and I knew that the upcoming custody battle was on his mind. He was concerned for Benjie, and I was too. It felt like one hurdle had been jumped but this next one might knock him down. I worried that he wouldn't be able to get back up, even with me pulling.

Chapter 16

Over the next month, Ryan and I spent as much time with Benjie as we could, relishing the closeness while we had it. Who knew what the future would bring? There was a real possibility that we would have to relinquish him to his mother and his stepfather soon. We wanted as much quality time as we could get, just in case. We thought it would be fun for me to teach him some basic karate moves. It gave us a chance to spend some quality time with him and teach him some things at the same time.

Benjie was an adorable student. I bought him a small gi and wrapped a white belt around his sturdy little waist. He frowned in concentration as I went through his first kata with him and he mimicked me perfectly. He loved our lessons and he always begged me to flip him and show him big kicks. I showed him a few simple sweep maneuvers and he delighted in taking his dad down with them. Benjie ate it up and we thought that we were doing something very positive for him.

That is, until one day when everything went wrong.

I was showing Benjie some straight punches and simple takedowns when he was distracted by the cartoon that came on TV. It was his favorite show and he turned his head for a brief second to watch the opening sequence. That's all it took. My closed fist accidentally connected with his eye and he stumbled back, tears spurting instantly. Then he started howling. Ryan was there in a second. He grabbed Benjie up in his arms and hugged him close, making soothing hush noises while he rubbed his back. I raced to Ryan's side and tipped up Benjie's face to inspect the damage. His little eye was already turning black and swelling.

I ran to the kitchen to get an icepack while Ryan and Benjie sat down on the loveseat. Benjie was calmer by then, his sobs turning to soft hiccupping spasms. He touched his puffy eye and said, "You really got me, Catie. I guess you won that round, huh?"

I chuckled and said, "We'll call it a draw. Here, put this on your eye. It'll be cold but it'll help."

He placed the pack on his eye and squirmed. "Ow. It is cold."

Ryan rubbed his son's back soothingly. "Just leave it on there for a while, my man. It'll feel better really soon."

We sat for about ten minutes with the icepack on Benjie's eye. He fidgeted and wiggled but held the pack in place. The eye looked quite a bit better once the swelling was down but it was still going to be black. And, of course, Nancy was coming to pick Benjie up in a few hours. Well, accidents happened, and it wasn't like I meant to hit the boy. I caressed the soft, downy curls on his head.

"Sorry about that, buddy. Are you ok? I really didn't mean to do it, you know. That's why we always concentrate in battle. A break in concentration can result in a break in your face."

He giggled. "It's ok, Catie. I'm a tough guy."

I laughed and hugged him. "You sure are."

The incident was soon forgotten and we enjoyed the rest of our afternoon. Benjie and his dad snuggled on the couch watching cartoons together. I busied myself tidying up the apartment. I wanted to give them some guy-time together.

Nancy arrived at five and that's when things got really ugly. She took one look at Benjie's bruised face and started screaming.

"What the hell happened to my son? What did you do to him?" she pushed herself into Ryan's face and shouted.

"Nancy, calm down. It was an accident. Catie was sparring with Benjie and she accidentally got him. That's all. It's over and he's fine."

"I'm fine, Mommy. Catie just broke my face," Benjie insisted, grabbing her hand and trying to pull her away from Ryan. I gripped Ryan's arm and tried to distance him from Nancy. Then she whirled on me.

"You bitch! You hit my son! How dare you hit my son! I'll teach you to touch other people's children, you abuser!"

She pushed me hard and I stumbled back. But I wouldn't retaliate. Not when Benjie was there, his little face crumpling, tears running down his chubby cheeks. He was very distraught by his mother's actions and I wouldn't do anything to upset him further.

"Nancy, calm down. You're scaring Benjie," I said levelly, never taking my eyes off her face.

She lunged and pushed me again, this time with even more of her strength. I was ready for that one, so I simply backed up and faced her, arms open and hands up. "I'm not going to fight you."

"No, but I'm going to kick your ass!" She closed her fist and hit me square in the nose. Blood trickled.

Ryan roared. "Nancy, what the hell are you doing? It was an accident, you bitch! You want me to arrest you for assault?"

She spun to face him again and a calculating smile spread on her face. "No, but I may want to press some charges of my own."

She whipped out her cell phone and dialed before Ryan could stop her. She barked, "I need an officer at 946 Charles St, apartment 8B. I have an assault to report."

Then she charged at me again, knocking me to the floor. As I fell, my head hit the coffee table and knocked it over. I saw stars. That did it. Benjie was screaming, Ryan was trying to shield him from the violence and get to me at the same time, and I had just about had enough. I shot up and locked Nancy in a basic hold, designed solely to restrain an attacker. She yowled like an injured cat and struggled. She was no match for my training, however, and even when she wriggled and bucked with all her might, I held firm. I wasn't hurting her; I was just keeping her from hurting me.

Seven minutes after her reckless phone call, the police showed up. Danny Gleason, Ryan's partner, was first on scene.

"What the hell is going on here?" he shouted, taking in the overturned furniture, Benjie shrieking in Ryan's arms, and Nancy and me on the floor still struggling against each other. Blood was running down my face from my nose. Nancy's thousand-dollar suit was torn at the shoulder.

"She attacked me and my son!" Nancy shouted, struggling to get up.

"Like hell she did, you lying bitch!" Ryan hollered. "You started the whole thing!"

Danny looked at me and said, "Caitlin, let her go."

I released Nancy and she wrenched herself away from me, yanking her shirt and skirt down. She glared at me and acted like the victim but I saw the vindictive smile on her face before she contorted it into an expression of pain.

"Catie, get up, turn around and put your hands, wrists together, palms out, behind your back. Slowly now." Danny moved toward me and cuffed my hands.

"What the hell, Gleason? It wasn't Catie's fault. Nancy attacked her, for Christ's sake! What the hell do you think you're doing?"

"She hit my son. I was just trying to protect him from that animal. I want her arrested for assaulting us both," Nancy spat.

"Ashford, I'm sorry. If she wants to press charges, I've got to take Catie in. I have to do this by the book."

"Goddamn it," Ryan growled. "You'd listen to her over me? I can tell you what happened here. It's not like she's saying. It didn't go down like that."

Danny walked over to Ryan and put a comforting hand on his shoulder. "Listen to me. If I don't do this right, she'll be shouting about preferential treatment and discrimination. You know that. Christ, you know her. I have to arrest Catie."

Ryan glared at Danny viciously and clutched a wailing Benjie to his chest. He nodded curtly. I stared at him and silently willed him to calm down. I didn't want things to get any worse. I'd just have to go with Danny and explain things in the car. Maybe they'd let me go.

Nancy stalked over to Ryan and held out her arms. "Give me my son, you fucker. You won't even see Benjie again until you get this abusive cunt out of your life. I won't have her attacking my son."

Ryan bellowed, "Watch your mouth, Nancy. You don't have to talk like that around Benjie!"

Nancy reached over and wrested him away from his dad and Benjie tried again to explain. "But, Mommy, Catie didn't mean to—"

"Benjamin, you listen to me. You won't be near that animal again. I won't let her hurt you anymore. Your head has been filled with this nonsense for long enough."

Benjie sniffed and started crying again. He laid his head on his mom's shoulder and sobbed his little heart out. My own heart felt like it was breaking and I could only imagine what was going on in Ryan's mind. The look on his face was murderous.

"Danny, I want charges pressed against this woman. In fact, I want a restraining order to keep her the hell away from my son."

Ryan looked at me entreatingly and then walked over to Danny. Lowering his voice, he asked, "Caitlin should press counter-charges. Look at her face. Nancy nailed her right in the nose."

Danny asked me, "Catie? Do you want to press charges?"

"If I do, what happens to Benjie? Can he stay with Ryan tonight?"

"Under the circumstances, Child Protective Services would be called in. Benjie would likely be placed in temporary care until the charges can be either investigated or dismissed."

"Then no. I won't have Benjie any more disrupted or upset than he is now. Just get this over with."

Danny nodded and turned to speak with Nancy.

"Are we through now?" she spat. Before Danny could respond, she stormed out of the door, holding her sobbing son in her arms. She threw her last comment over her shoulder. "I'll have my lawyer contact you with my statement."

"Bye, Daddy. Bye, Catie. I'm sorry." Benjie's tear-streaked face disappeared around the door frame and his sobs echoed down the hallway as he and Nancy left the building.

Danny waited until the sobs had disappeared and grabbed my arm. "Let's go, Catie. Ryan, you can come down to the precinct when I've gotten Catie processed, ok? You stay here until then."

"Goddamn it, Danny! Don't do this. She's gone now. Can't you just let her go?"

"You know I can't. I'm sorry, Ryan. I really am. Don't worry. I'll take care of Catie for you." He moved toward the apartment door, leading me by my elbow.

"Wait a God-damned minute, would you?" Ryan grabbed a towel and wiped away most of the blood from my face. He murmured, "I'm so sorry, sweetheart. I'll figure out how to get you out of this, ok?"

I nodded and allowed myself to be led to Danny's squad car.

"Here, let me take off those cuffs. It's the least I can do. But I have to put them back on once we get to the precinct, ok?"

I nodded in gratitude and Danny removed the cuffs.

"Catie, I'm sorry about all this," Danny said as we drove to the station.

"It's not your fault. She's a royal bitch though, huh?"

"You said it. I'd like to kick her ass but then they'd get me for police brutality." He winked at me.

"Yeah, they frown on that sort of stuff."

He chuckled. "Listen, I want to thank you."

"For what?"

"For being with Ryan. He really loves you."

"I love him too." It was an odd place to realize that you loved someone, in the back of a cop car, but I did. It hit me like a ton of bricks. If I thought I loved him before; now I knew I did.

Four hours later, I was processed, fingerprinted and bailed out by Ryan, who stormed into the precinct like he was staging a coup. He barged into the office of his supervisor and pulled every string he could to get me released. He had brought his attorney with him and while Ryan worked to get me out, the lawyer sat with me and took down my side of the story. The three of us left together and we drove to a diner downtown to talk.

"So Ms. Ashford-Raines refuses to drop the charges of assault and battery. She's claiming you not only hit her but you beat Benjamin as well. She is citing abuse by you over an extended period of time and she's alleging that you are a danger to her son. She has filed a restraining order against you. According to the order, you aren't allowed within a thousand feet of her son at any time."

"What? That's ridiculous. Catie would never deliberately hurt Benjie. She was just teaching him karate. It was an accident." Ryan scowled fiercely.

"Be that as it may, the order stands. When we go to court, Ms. Ashford-Raines will undoubtedly try to use this against you in her case to move the boy across state lines. I would recommend a break in your relationship with Ms. Edison for now until things settle down. If you don't, she will certainly be in a position to claim sole custody of the boy, citing this incident and your continued relationship with Ms. Edison as a reason to keep you away from him."

"But, damn it, that's not fair. Catie is a wonderful person and she's been so good to Benjie, to both of us. I won't shove her aside just to satisfy Nancy's sick need to destroy me. Nancy may not want me anymore, but I'll be damned if she can decide who I have in my life. She can't control that. She made her choice."

"I'm afraid that she has every right to control who Benjamin has in his life. As a parent she needs to act in his best interest and she doesn't feel that it is in Benjamin's best interest to be near your girlfriend."

"So I'm just supposed to stop seeing Catie to make her happy?"

I interjected. "No, you're supposed to stop seeing me so you can be with Benjie. Ryan, I'm not going to allow you to choose between me and your son. He's more important. You need to be with him and he needs to be with you. I'm not going to be responsible for driving you two apart. I couldn't live with myself if I did."

"But—"

"We can always appeal later. For now, just get Benjie away from that awful woman. You and I know the truth and that's all that matters."

The attorney nodded. He looked at Ryan, whose face was filled with pain and barely-suppressed anger. He lifted his gaze to meet mine and sighed.

"I hate that woman."

I knew. I hated her, too, but it was the only way to get Benjie with his dad. I would willingly make the sacrifice. I understood love now and I would never be selfish with it.

Ryan stood, hugged me and said, "Come on, I'll get you home."

We drove to my apartment in silence. I held his hand but my touch barely registered to him. He didn't even glance at me and his hand was limp in mine. I knew how tough this must be for him but there was really no other option. Besides, things would be resolved soon, wouldn't they?

Ryan walked me to my door and said, "I probably shouldn't come in."

"No, probably not. Listen, I'm so sorry. I never meant for any of this to happen. I'll never forgive myself if I cause Benjie to be taken away from you."

"That's not going to happen. I won't allow it to happen and one day we'll be together again. All three of us. Soon. I promise."

He kissed me tenderly, careful not to bump my swollen nose, and said, "I'll see you later, ok?"

I nodded and shut the door. Every cell in my body rebelled against the action. It felt wrong to shut him out of my life. I went to my freezer, pulled out some ice and rubbed it on my throbbing nose. Being a karate student, I had been punched in the face before—countless times—but this blow seemed to sting worse.

I went to my bedroom and flopped down on my bed. I had finally been ready to make a life with someone, but here I was, alone again, and the whole thing sucked.

Chapter 17

My phone rang at 9:00 the next morning. I had called off work because my face was bruised, my nose was swollen and one eye had turned black. I really didn't feel like giving the office gossips more fuel for their fire, so I planned on icing my face for a few hours today and experimenting with makeup to cover my injuries.

"Hello?" I answered.

"Hi, sweetheart. I miss you." Ryan! Relief and love flooded me. I wasn't sure when I would hear from him again. His warm, masculine voice was a balm on my ragged soul.

"Oh, Ryan, I miss you, too. What are you doing calling me? Won't you get in trouble?"

"Catie, she can't control who I talk to on the phone. The attorney says we shouldn't see each other but I'll be damned if they tell me who I can or can't talk to."

"Well, ok, but what if they ask for phone records?"

"I have a friend who works at the phone company, remember?" I heard his grin through the phone and I was relieved. I had been so worried about him after he dropped me off last night but I was too scared of complicating things to call him. It was wonderful to hear his voice.

"So, what's the latest word? Do I get to see you sometime soon?"

"They postponed trial, sweetheart. They want me and Nancy to go through remediation before we go to court to see if we can come up with an agreement. But I'm afraid she won't drop the charges against you unless I agree to relinquish custody to her and allow her to cross state lines with Benjie. I won't do that."

"Don't agree to that. I'll be fine. The attorney said that I have a good shot at the charges being dismissed at my court date anyway. After all, I've never been in any trouble and I have some character witnesses we can call. Don't worry about me. Just work on getting Benjie back."

"I know, but I feel horrible that you've been dragged into this. It's not fair to you."

"Well, look what I put you through during the first six months of our relationship. Now it's your turn to exact revenge on me. Seems to me we're even, although I never gave you a criminal record, " I smirked, trying to keep it lighthearted for his sake.

He laughed. "I think I actually owe you one. At least I never left one of our dates with bumps or bruises."

"You can make it up to me later. For now, let's concentrate on giving that bitch what she deserves."

"What did I ever do to deserve you?"

"You got horny at a bar one night, remember?"

"Oh, yeah. That was it. Damn me and my hormones, anyway."

"You know, I think I've used that exact line before," I giggled. This was nice, in a weird kind of way. We were apart but I had never felt closer to him. We were a team, albeit a long-distance one at the moment.

"Yeah? Huh. Great minds think alike. I miss you."

"I think I've used that one too. So, what would we be doing right now if we were together?"

"Hmm. Let me see. I'd make you breakfast in bed. Do you like omelets?"

"I sure do. Do you know how to make omelets?" I asked, intrigued. He always seemed pretty handy in the kitchen.

"Nope. But I can make scrambled eggs and heat up canned corned-beef hash." I heard his grin through the phone line and thought that it was too bad he wasn't here. I could think of other things to do in the morning.

"Yeah? Sounds good. So, after breakfast, what would we do?"

"Well, since I just served breakfast in bed, I'd clear the dishes and fix dessert."

"What kind of dessert do you have after breakfast in bed?"

"Sexy dessert."

"*Oh.*"

"Yeah."

I closed my eyes and imagined it for a moment, his warm hard frame next to mine, his breath tickling me as he trailed kisses down my body. I could feel his arms around me and his hands on me. I sighed. He sighed.

"I miss you."

"I miss you too. We'll get through this, Catie. I swear. Then it'll be the three of us."

I smiled, murmured good-bye and hung up the phone. Life was so unfair. I was angry at Nancy for trying to ruin what was promising to be a wonderful relationship. And why was she doing it? It was bad enough that she was trying to take Benjie away from his dad just so she could move away with her awful new husband, but why would she try to ruin what Ryan and I had with each other?

It occurred to me that Nancy might be jealous. Maybe things weren't that great with her new man. Maybe she missed Ryan. She sure had a hell of a bargaining chip. How awful that Benjie was being used as a pawn by his mom to get back with his dad. He was just a child and he was being jerked around by the person who was supposed to protect him. I wondered if Ryan had figured this out yet. Probably not. He was right in the thick of things and I doubted he had been able to distance himself from the situation long enough to rationally think about things. Still, the lawyer would be fighting and I was confident that justice would prevail. The judge had to see how much Benjie needed his dad.

Over the course of the next few weeks, Ryan and I talked on the phone but we didn't see each other. He kept me updated on the progress of the custody matter and he said it was slow going. The remediation had stopped without any sort of resolution; now the actual hearing was underway, and what normally took one court date to decide was still ongoing. Both lawyers kept filing continuances and rebuttals.

"Nancy is trying to say that with her husband's financial resources, she's better equipped to take care of Benjie. That's bullshit. She just wants to hang onto her precious money. If she gave him to me, she'd have to pay me child support. I'm not sure she gives a shit about Benjie at all. It was always the money with her."

The next day he complained, "She's trying to tell the judge that my job is so emotionally taxing that Benjie would be in a constant state of mental stress worrying about me. She says she can provide him a more stable environment than I can simply because of the work I do. What the hell is that all about? It's my job to make everyone safe and that includes Benjie. Does she honestly think I'd take that responsibility lightly?"

And then, "Nancy said that people in my life are known abusers and have hurt Benjie on numerous occasions. I'd like to hurt her for talking about you that way. The judge wouldn't even let me explain. I about lost it and the lawyer said it didn't make me look good. It's so hard to keep calm through all this horseshit."

Next it was, "My lawyer said that Nancy will allow Benjie to spend summers with me if I sign an agreement that I break all contact with you. I told him to fuck himself."

By then, I had heard enough and tried to calm him down. "Ryan, you can't do that. You know something? I think she's jealous of us. That's all it is. She's hell-bent on keeping us apart because I think she regrets leaving you. You know how they say the grass is always greener? Well, that cow is chewing her cud and having a hard time swallowing it right now."

"I think you might be right. I don't know why I didn't see it before. But wouldn't she toss over her new husband and try to get me back? Why would she bother to stay with him and take Benjie away?"

"Because she can't back down now. She's a proud person. There's no way she'd admit she made a mistake. The only way for her to fix it, in her mind, is to destroy you to build herself up. And if she has Benjie, she always has a bond with you, not to mention a way to manipulate you."

"Damn her. If she thinks she can manipulate me, she's got another thing coming. I'll call you later."

Ryan hung up abruptly. I was worried. What was he planning? I put in a call to the attorney's office just to prepare him for dealing with Ryan's temper, but all I got was his voicemail. It seemed Ryan had gotten to him first.

The rest of that day passed slowly. To distract myself from the worry I felt, I decided to call my girls and have a night out. I needed some levity.

We met at our favorite bar and everything was still the same. The "Beer" sign still shone in its lopsided way, the same old men leered at us when we entered and Ernie the bartender still made the best screwdrivers in town.

We sat at our regular table and squabbled amongst ourselves to decide who would get the first round. Kelly lost and she got up to get us our drinks. I sat with Heidi who was looking pensive. Her normally happy demeanor seemed somewhat dulled and I was concerned.

"Heidi, what's wrong? You seem sad." I slung my arm around her and hugged her to me.

"Peter asked me to marry him."

"What?" I screeched. Heidi, our perpetual virgin, was engaged to be married?

"Shhh. I haven't decided yet."

"But you guys are wonderful together. What is there to decide?"

"Well, I'm just not sure I'm ready to give myself to a man yet."

"Is that all? You're scared of that?"

"I didn't say I was scared. I just don't know if I'm ready." She frowned at me and I smiled. Oh, to have her problems.

"Well, do you love him?" I asked, grinning at her.

"Yes, I do," she answered instantly.

"And does he love you?"

"He says he does."

"So, have a lengthy engagement. Try it on for size. There's nothing that says you have to get married immediately after getting engaged."

"No, there isn't, is there?" She seemed to brighten a little after that. Kelly returned with our drinks and we all toasted each other. Heidi told Kelly her news and they squealed and jumped up and down like schoolgirls. Afterward, we all settled in to do some serious talking and drinking. It had been a while, and while I normally didn't discuss my love life with anyone, I found myself wanting to share the burden, just to get things off my chest. While I pounded my drink, I told my girls of the latest developments.

"Do you want me to go find her and beat the shit out of her for you?" my stripper-turned-paralegal asked me. She had gotten a job at a local law office recently and I was happy for her. Pandering herself to lawyers was much classier than doing it to a bunch of horny men.

"No, I think I'll pass. I don't think that would help things much. I'm just upset. Ryan is a great dad and she'd throw that relationship away just to serve her own purposes."

"What about you two?" Kelly asked, concerned.

"We talk on the phone but we haven't been able to see each other. I miss him but I won't jeopardize the case he has right now."

"You know what you need?" Heidi asked.

I smirked. "Let me guess, another hook-up?"

"No, another drink." Heidi handed me the rest of her screwdriver and called to Ernie to make us three more, doubles this time.

We drank and danced, talked and laughed. Before I knew it, I was drunk. Really drunk. Normally I can hold my liquor but the stress had obviously gotten to me, and so had all the screwdrivers. I was wasted. By midnight, I was seeing double and weaving on my feet. It was time to go home and sleep it off. I declined the offer of a taxi and abandoned my car in the parking lot. I figured if I had some fresh air and a chance to walk it off, I'd be fine.

Perhaps two blocks from the bar, I became aware of car lights following me. I walked faster, glancing behind me warily. Even intoxicated, I could tell when I liked a situation and when I didn't. My senses prickled. My karate training kicked in. I was instantly hyperaware of my surroundings—nothing escaped my guard.

The car eased closer and I stopped to face it. No sense in allowing a potential attacker to have my undefended back. The car window rolled down and I could see a man's face in the dashboard light, although I couldn't see it clearly. My eyes were fuzzy and I had double-vision from all the vodka I consumed. Damn alcohol. It wasn't making my self-defense easy, that was for sure.

"Hop in. I'll take you home."

"Like hell, asshole. I can get myself home," I snarled, easing myself into a position that would allow me to quickly defend myself from my attacker.

"Catie, come on. You know you're safe with me."

"Who is that? Oh, my god—Ryan?" The car was a police cruiser and the two-headed man behind the wheel was my man.

I yanked open the door and threw myself across the seat into his arms. They encircled me and our mouths met recklessly. It was so good to feel his warmth, so good to see his face, even if he appeared to have four eyes at the moment. I had missed him so much.

"What are you doing out here at this hour?" he asked me, confusion and concern making him frown.

"I was out with my girls. I'm a little drunk, ok—a lot drunk, so I'm walking home. Was walking home. Then you showed up. What are you doing here? And why do you have two sets of eyes?"

He grinned devilishly. "Sweetheart, I'm on midnight patrol tonight. You're lucky it was me who found you. Of course, you were pretty scary with your 'I'll get myself home, asshole' routine."

"Self-defense 101. The crude language adds a nice touch, don't you think?"

"Sure does, but not coming from such a pretty girl. You're a tempting little badass, you know that?"

"Take me home, Ryan. I'll show you tempting."

He drove me home quickly. I touched him the whole way, reveling in the contact that had been missing for so long.

He ushered me inside and pushed me against the door, covering my body with his and showing me exactly how much he missed me. His lips trailed kisses along my jaw and my throat, inciting moans of pleasure from me. I burned for him. I needed him. He spread my legs and settled himself between them, pushing his knee up against my center. I groaned and begged, "Can't you come to bed with me?"

"I can't stay long. I'm on duty."

"Don't worry. This won't take long."

We raced to my bedroom and our coupling was explosive—hard, fast and perfect. Afterward, we lay sated, panting, touching each other as if to make sure it wasn't a dream. A chance meeting that ended up like this was the stuff of fairytales, or good porn, and we hated to end it. But duty called and Ryan's radio went off just as we got dressed again.

"I have to go."

"I know."

"Marry me, Catie." He looked at me solemnly. "I'd go down on one knee but I haven't had a chance to get the ring yet. It's still being sized at the jeweler's."

I stammered, "But, Benjie and the lawyers and Nancy—what about Nancy?"

"Let me worry about it. I've already talked to my attorney about this. Catie, this is going to work. Just trust me. I'm going to get Benjie and we'll be a family. That is, if you'll have me."

"Oh, Ryan. I'd love to marry you. I just don't want to ruin your chances to get Benjie permanently."

"You won't. I promise. Just wait and see. We'll be happy."

"Of that, I have no doubt. But are you sure?"

"Of you? Absolutely, sweetheart. I've got to go. But I'll be back." He kissed me and dashed out the door, radio squawking and squealing.

I hugged my arms around myself and sighed. I was deliriously happy but seriously worried. What if this was the end of Ryan's custody battle with Nancy? What if this caused him to lose his case? Oh why did happiness have to be so complicated? I slumped into bed and was soon sleeping, despite my worries.

In the morning, I woke up to soft kisses and a masculine voice in my ear saying, "Good morning, beautiful."

Warm hands trailed down my sides, across my stomach and over my face. I opened my eyes and saw Ryan's face—the face of the man I'd spend the rest of my life with.

"Hmmm, good morning. Do you always wake up the drunks you cart home this way?"

"No, just the good-looking ones who agree to be my wife."

"About that… are you sure? What exactly did the attorney say?"

"He said that we could disprove the abuse allegations. He also thinks that if we're married, we'll appear more stable and beneficial for Benjie."

"Please tell me that's not the only reason you asked me to marry you, Ryan." I frowned. My insecurities were getting the best of me once again. Would he really ask me to marry him just to get custody of his son?

"Please tell me you didn't just ask me that question, Caitlin. You know me better than that." His jubilant mood of a moment before vanished.

"I'm sorry. I didn't mean it."

"I think you might have. And let me tell you something. I don't play games. I know what I want and I know how I feel. I would never abuse the feelings of one person for the sake of another. It's all or nothing with me, and if you don't know how I feel about you by now, maybe I asked you to be my wife too soon."

He started to get up and I clung to his arm. "Wait, ok? I'm sorry."

He sat back down and gathered me close. "Do you want to know how I feel?"

Instead of waiting for my response, he said, "You mean the world to me. I was miserable without you. All I could think about was holding you again, talking to you again, looking in your eyes and telling you that I couldn't live without you. I drove my lawyer crazy with questions about when I could see you again. Sweetheart, I have three thoughts when I wake up in the morning. You know what they are?"

"What?" I asked, mesmerized by the sound of his voice telling me everything I always wanted to hear.

"First, I think of Benjie and hope he's ok. Second, I think of you and hope you're ok. Third, I think of how wonderful it'll be when we can all be together."

"Ryan, I love you."

"And you know what? At night when I go to bed, I think of those same three things. I think of those things all day, every day. I love you, and I need you, and not because of any goddamned custody battle."

He crushed me to him and held me close. I sighed and snuggled into his embrace. But suddenly, he pulled away and said, "I have something for you."

He hopped off the bed, reached into his pocket, and got down on one knee. A ring box was nestled in his palm and he opened it with a flick of his other hand. Inside was a gorgeous emerald-cut diamond ring.

"Fresh from the jeweler's. I waited outside their door this morning for them to open up. I hounded the jeweler and held him at gunpoint until he finished sizing it."

I held out my hand and he slid on the ring. I gazed down at the promise on my finger and smiled. It was a perfect fit, just like us.

Chapter 18

We met with the lawyer the following day to discuss our plans and the new strategy. The first order of business was to get the assault charges against me dropped. The attorney worked with the local D.A. and managed to get the assault reduced to simple harassment. Still, I'd have to go to court and fight the new charge. I had pleaded not-guilty, and to get my case dismissed I'd have to go to trial.

It was a rainy day and the dreary atmosphere suited my mood. If I was convicted, I could lose my job and my man. I wasn't even going to think about the jail time I could serve.

Ryan and I walked into the courtroom holding hands. It looked just like the courtrooms did on TV, all wood and gleaming brass railings and a raised platform holding the judge's bench front and center. The judge hadn't arrived yet and there was just a smattering of people in the room: bailiffs, attorneys, and court reporters getting warmed up for the action. Ryan and I walked to the defense's table and our lawyer stood up to greet us. We sat down and conferred quietly with him. He seemed to think that we had a good chance at coming out victorious. We just smiled at him and received congratulations on our recent engagement. Then Nancy walked in.

She played the part of victim to perfection. She was dressed in a somber suit. Her hair was drab and her expression was one of pain and anguish. She refused to meet my gaze and leaned into her lawyer's side as if she was afraid to even be in the same room as me. What a crock of shit.

Ryan tensed and the look in his eyes was deadly. He started to rise as if to confront her but our attorney grabbed his arm and stopped him before he could completely stand up. Being aggressive in any way could only hurt our chances, he advised. He was confident in our case and his very posture showed it. He felt we had nothing to worry about.

At his request, Dr. Ross wrote a statement about my character, and Kelly and Heidi each contributed one too. Isamu wrote a statement about my training as well as the whole philosophy behind karate and the values he instilled in his students. Our attorney felt this was a slam-dunk win.

The judge walked in and called us to order. My heart rate accelerated and I felt my pulse throb. Ryan squeezed my hand and the lawyer patted my shoulder. It was time.

Nancy's lawyer started first, painting a picture of a wife who was tossed aside by her vicious cop-husband and later abused by her husband's new trollop of a girlfriend. He told the jury that he'd prove beyond a shadow of a doubt that this poor victim was attacked simply because she was trying to get her precious son away from someone who would abuse him. Ryan cursed quietly under his breath. Our lawyer laid a gentle hand on his arm and murmured to him.

When it was our turn, our attorney stood up and said few words. But one thing he did say seemed to reverberate around the courtroom. He said, "I will prove that this supposed victim is actually a manipulative con-artist who is punishing her ex-husband. She is punishing him for moving on and finding a life with a warm, caring, supportive woman who would move Heaven and Earth to see the man she loves and his son happy. This woman has excellent character, and any man would be proud to make her his own."

The police blotter was read, and true to his word, Danny had taken care of me. In his official report, he described in detail the living room as it was when he entered it, the blood pouring out of my nose and the hold that I had Nancy in. He explained that it was a classic move that both policemen and karate students were taught to use to restrain, not harm, their attackers. He stated that Benjie was crying that about how his black eye was an accident and that he was fine. Danny was eventually called to the stands to verify the information in the police report and asked if he was aware of the issues that his partner and Nancy were having.

"Yes, I am. But I had to do the job so there were no problems later. If someone presses charges, no matter what I think, I have to make an arrest."

"And what did you think about it?"

"It was crap. Catie would never hurt anyone. Nancy didn't have a mark on her, but Catie was bleeding through the nose and had a goose-egg on the back of her head."

"Objection, your Honor," the prosecuting attorney jumped up and sputtered.

"Sustained. Please refrain from asking the witness what he thinks. Stick to pertinent facts."

"It was pertinent," Danny muttered as he stepped down.

The next witness was Ryan. He was sworn in and seated.

"Mr. Ashford, can you tell us what happened that night?"

"Caitlin and I were in my living room with my son Benjie, teaching him some karate moves. Catie has been in karate for over twenty years and she was trying to teach him some things. He loved it. But his cartoons came on the TV and he turned his face for just a minute. It threw off Catie's aim and she accidentally struck him in the eye. He cried, but we iced it and hugged him, and he was fine. The swelling was minimal but his eye was blackened."

"So, how did your ex-wife and Ms. Edison end up on the floor, bloodied and restrained?"

"Well, when Nancy got to my house to pick Benjie up, she saw his eye and started screaming. We tried to explain what happened, but she got in my face, and then in Catie's face when she tried to calm Nancy down. Benjie was getting upset and Caitlin saw that. Catie told Nancy that she was scaring Benjie but Nancy wouldn't listen. Nancy pushed Catie twice but Catie refused to engage in any physical contact. Nancy hit Catie in the nose and charged at her, knocking her down and causing her to hit her head. So Catie got her in a hold and waited until the police came."

"So Catie never struck Nancy?"

"No sir, she did not."

I was called to the witness stand and the lawyer got down to business.

"Ms. Edison, what happened the night that you were arrested?"

"Well, it's the same as what Mr. Ashford told you. I was teaching Benjie some basic karate moves and his face accidentally met my fist."

"You didn't mean to strike him?"

"Of course not. I love Benjie. He's a great kid."

"And you've never struck or hurt Benjie before?"

"No, never. We have a lot of fun when we're together."

"So how would you describe your relationship with him?"

"We're friends. I love his father and I hope to be a part of his family one day."

"What sort of relationship do you have with Mr. Ashford's ex-wife, Nancy?"

"I don't have one."

"So why did you hit her?"

"I didn't. I wanted to. She was upsetting Benjie terribly while she was screaming at me and Ryan. But I knew if I hurt her, it would just upset Benjie, so I didn't hit her back when she attacked me."

"But you and Ms. Ashford-Raines ended up on the floor together."

"Well, yes. But that's because she charged at me, punched me in the nose and knocked me down onto the ground. Then I got mad."

"So, you struck her then?"

"No, I put her in a hold so she couldn't strike me. It also tied up my hands so I couldn't hit her, even if I wanted to." I looked over at Nancy smugly. The bitch had to know I was in control of the situation during her supposed attack on me and now in the courtroom.

Throughout the proceedings, Nancy's face got redder and redder.

When her lawyer questioned me, he tried to shake my testimony but it didn't work. Their chance at a conviction became slimmer and slimmer, especially when the character statements were called into evidence and read aloud for the court.

The jury went to deliberate but they weren't gone long. They came back with a verdict of not guilty five minutes after they left.

Ryan grabbed me and spun me jubilantly. He whooped and hollered and squeezed me until I thought my ribs were going to break. Our lawyer smiled and shook both our hands. We walked out of the courtroom holding hands.

Our bliss didn't last long because Nancy charged at us and snarled, "This isn't over. You'll never see your son again, you bastard. Not if this tramp is in your life."

"Nancy, why do you hate me? You don't want him. Why won't you let him have some happiness?" I asked her softly.

"Stay out of this, you bitch, or I'll have you arrested again."

"For what? I was just leaving and you came up and verbally attacked us. Seems to me like we have more grounds for an arrest than you do."

Danny walked to our sides, his official uniform starched and pressed neatly. His badge gleamed in the sunlight. "She's right, you know, Nancy. I'd leave quietly if I were you or I'll have to write you a ticket for disturbing the peace and disorderly conduct, not to mention harassment."

She spun on her heel and stomped down the courthouse steps. Victory was ours, at least for the day. But, like Nancy said, this wasn't over.

Chapter 19

With my criminal record gone and my engagement to Ryan official, things seemed to settle down, for the time being anyway. The restraining order was dropped and I quietly moved my things into Ryan's much larger apartment. We still had the custody hearing to live through but Ryan felt like we had a fighting chance. I could be there for Benjie when Ryan worked late-nights and we would rarely need daycare due to our work schedules. Our lives seemed to intermingle splendidly. However, I had yet to introduce Ryan to Gran and I was dreading it.

Since Gran's revelation, I hadn't spoken to her much. Even though I had forgiven her and decided to control my emotions regarding the whole issue, her blatant rejection still stung. Although I no longer required her approval for anything, I still wanted it.

It was Ryan's idea that we go visit Gran together. That way, if she got too out of hand, I'd have some support. I was leery of the whole idea because he didn't know my Gran the way I did, but he insisted.

"Sweetheart, what's the worst she can do? I'm a cop. I can arrest her, for Pete's sake."

We drove to her stately home one evening in autumn. The leaves had already all dropped into crisp, colorful piles that had yet to be raked. They lined the wide streets and covered the deep front yards of Gran's neighborhood and gave the grounds a patchwork quilt appearance. We drove up the lighted drive and parked in front of Gran's front steps. I adjusted my hair, my coat and my dignity, and grasped Ryan's hand like a lifeline as we walked to the door. I balked as we got closer, and he tugged my hand and forced me forward. He chuckled a little.

"What's the matter, sweetheart? Last-minute jitters?"

"No, I've had them a while," I insisted. "You don't know my Gran."

"Yeah, but I'm trained to deal with difficult witnesses. And besides, she'll love me."

I wasn't so sure. She didn't even love me, but it was too late now. Ryan knocked with the brass doorknocker and the door opened.

Gran looked irritated. She was not dressed for company and I regretted not telling her we'd be coming over. I wanted the element of surprise on my side and I knew I needed all the tricks I had up my sleeves in order to leave with even an ounce of pride, but my confidence was shaken after I saw the look on her face.

"What is it, Caitlin? Who is this?" She frowned at both of us and I felt myself shrinking to about two inches tall. Power or not, the old crone still scared the shit out of me.

"Gran, can we come in?"

She gestured and we entered the sumptuous foyer. She led us into the sitting room off the entryway and we sat dutifully. I felt like I was twelve again.

"Would you care for a drink?" Gran asked, a thoroughbred to the core.

"No, that's ok. We really came to talk," I explained.

"Talk? At this hour? About what?" she scowled at me and Ryan.

"Mrs. Danforth, my name is Ryan Ashford. I'm a police officer with the Pittston police department, and I—"

"Caitlin Paige Edison, what have you done? Why are the police here talking to me? I always knew you'd end up in trouble. What have you done?" she repeated. Her face was growing red and the frown lines on her forward appeared super-glued in place.

"Gran, it's not like that. Ryan is my boyfriend. I thought I should introduce you."

"Well, actually, Mrs. Danforth, we—"

I elbowed Ryan discreetly to stop him. Gran had to get used to the idea in small doses. He had no idea about the wrath of my grandmother.

Gran was not to be fooled or coddled. She glared at the both of us and sat back imperiously in her favored wing back chair. "Are you pregnant?"

"What? Gran—no! How could you even ask me something like that?" I gasped in horror.

"It seems to be the trend nowadays. Get pregnant, move in together, and forget all about honor and tradition. I assumed that since you have no problem shacking up with a man, you'd be fine with all the other things that women of loose morals do."

"Now, wait a minute, you—" I sputtered, angry beyond belief. I may have had sex before marriage with a total of two guys in ten years, but I didn't have loose morals.

Ryan put a restraining arm around me and said, "Mrs. Danforth, I'd appreciate it if you wouldn't talk about my fiancée that way." He smiled at her then, a triumphant, confident smile, and silently dared her to try it again.

"Your fiancée? Since when? Caitlin, how long have you known this boy? And what about Michael?"

"Ma'am, I'm afraid that's none of your business. What is your business is that Catie has agreed to be my wife and I promise you I'll take good care of her. I'd appreciate it if you'd give her the respect of her privacy when it comes to details."

"Gran, Ryan and I have been dating for months now. And I love him, I really do. Besides, I'm through with Michael. It's over. We've been done for a long time now. Why do you have such a problem with that?"

"You barely know this boy. And why haven't I met him before? I suppose now you want me to pay for this wedding and I don't even know if I approve of the groom. Why, I've never even met him before today. I expected better from you, Caitlin. I should think you'd understand why I have a problem with this—whatever it is."

"Gran, Ryan is wonderful, and so is his son." I looked at her smugly.

"Son? Catie, what are you trying to prove? Don't you have any idea of what you're getting into? How do you know he's not some man trying to marry his babysitter?"

"Excuse me?"

"Well, I think the last thing you need is someone who is trying to saddle you with a child who isn't yours. You can barely take care of yourself."

"I know what this is about, Gran, and you aren't being fair. I'm entitled to make my own decisions. I'm twenty-eight years old and I have been living on my own since I was eighteen. You have no right to tell me what I should and shouldn't do, or who I should or shouldn't see. I think I'm doing just fine, without your help."

"Of course you're entitled to make your own decisions. But

you're making the wrong ones. I told Shelly the same thing before she married Keith and just look what happened," she challenged, eyes as cold as ice. I could only imagine her heart was that way as well. Interesting, too, that she no longer referred to my parents as 'your mom and dad'. It was now Shelly and Keith.

"Mom and Dad loved each other, and they loved you too. It's not their fault the plane crashed. Will you stop blaming them for something that happened almost twenty years ago and let them rest? And while you're at it, let me rest too. I know you can't stand the sight of me. I know you didn't want to raise me. So now I'm grown, let me live my life. You always said to let the past stay in the past. Why can't you take your own advice?"

I got up and motioned for Ryan to do the same. He stood and somberly gazed at Gran. "Mrs. Danforth, I love Catie. I can't promise what the future will bring but I can promise that I'll take care of her as best I can for as long as I live. She's an adult and if you don't start treating her like one, you'll lose her. Don't make her choose between two people she loves very much. It'll hurt her. I hope you'll give us your blessing and I hope we'll see you at our wedding."

We strode out of the house, leaving Gran behind in her wing chair, her face and her heart set in stone, arms folded tightly across her chest. As much as that poignant vignette bothered me, I also felt liberated. Ryan loved me and, for once, someone had stood up to her with me. It felt great. Michael always agreed with Gran and contradicted me whenever we went head-to-head. But times were changed, and Ryan and I were a team. Gran wasn't half as scary and threatening when I had my teammate by my side.

"That went well," he remarked.

"Actually, it went better than I expected it to," I told him, smirking.

"Really? She's quite something. I had no idea that she was that ... rigid."

"She's just scared of losing control again. She lost control over my mom and look what happened. Now, she's losing control of me, and she's afraid. You know what?" I asked him.

"What, sweetheart?"

"Seeing her that way, all upset? It showed me that she's human, not some dictatorial matron who smacks her pupils with rulers when they don't obey. She can't scare me anymore. Thank you, Ryan, for being there when I faced her again."

"Glad to be of service, Miss. But I think she hates me."

"No, she doesn't. She actually admires spunk. But give her time. She'll come around eventually. Hmmm—maybe she'll even like me. I'm full of spunk."

We held hands and walked to the car, smiling. One hurdle down, a few more to go.

Over the next few weeks, I busied myself with wedding plans. I went dress shopping, picked out invitations and planned our reception. We got Ryan, Benjie and Danny fitted for matching tuxes. Ryan was arranging our honeymoon. All I knew was that we were going someplace tropical; beyond that it was a mystery.

At night, we cuddled on the couch and watched our favorite shows, and we learned to cook exotic dishes together. Our favorite was Thai cuisine. Before too long, we mastered curry and chicken tempura and all kinds of palate-tempting foods. We got Benjie as often as we could and made tents in the living room to sleep in together. Benjie seemed to thrive in our company and we truly enjoyed him. He made our house a home.

We even heard from Gran, although it was just a phone call cautioning me about hurricane season in tropical climes. Gran acted as though she was scared to death of our plane crashing on our way to the honeymoon and she did everything she could think of to dissuade us. Well, at least Gran was calling me. I thought it was a little strange that she was pretending to care, however. Ryan told me not to look a gift horse in the mouth. I told him that although my Gran certainly reminded me of a certain barn animal, I wouldn't dare get anywhere near her mouth for fear of getting bitten.

Life was idyllic, and for the first time in a long time, I was in a good place. It was too bad karma had a way of kicking people down a notch or two if things got too good to be true.

Chapter 20

Two months before the wedding, I was sitting at home in our living room debating on centerpiece arrangements for the guest tables at our reception, when the doorbell rang. I wasn't expecting anyone and I was curious to know who would show up at our apartment at eight o'clock in the evening. Ryan wasn't expected home for another hour and Gran never came calling here. She frowned on my living arrangements and refused to visit me. Maybe it was Kelly or Heidi, I mused.

I hopped lightly to my feet and walked to the door. I looked through the peephole and my heart gave a huge thump in trepidation. What was *he* doing here?

I answered the door and said, "Michael! What a surprise. What's going on?"

"Hi, Catie. Can I come in?"

"Sure." I motioned him inside.

He looked fantastic. His blond was freshly-cut and he was clean-shaven. He wore a black t-shirt and faded jeans that sat just right on his trim hips. He smelled wonderful. The cologne assaulted my nose as he stepped into the living room, bringing back ten years of memories. I wondered what he wanted and I gazed up into his blue eyes curiously.

"So, what brings you here and how did you know where I live?" I asked him.

"Your Gran told me where you were. I, uh, stopped by your apartment a while back but you weren't there. The new tenants told me you moved out. So, I called Gran to find out where you went. This is a step up from our old apartment, huh?"

"We like it here. So, why did you track me down? What's wrong?"

"Let's sit down, ok? I want to do this sitting down."

"Do what? Michael, what is going on here? Where's your wife?"

"I didn't marry Charlotte."

"What? What happened?" I was concerned for Michael, and confused. Why would he bother coming to tell me this? Well, I conceded, maybe he needed a friend to talk things over with. And seeing Michael didn't have the same effect it used to on me. Since I agreed to become Ryan's wife, I knew what love was. Michael was no longer the one I pined for. He was simply a friend and I would always be there for my friends.

"Catie, I couldn't marry her, not when my feelings are so strong for someone else."

"Ok, you're confusing me. How many women do you have in

your life, Casanova?" I teased.

"Just one." He stared at me somberly, and I squirmed. He was acting a little too intensely for my comfort. Something was up and I didn't like it.

"And when do I get to hear about this one? Where did you meet her?"

"I think you already know her quite well. Honey, it's you. I've been a real ass."

My jaw snapped open so far that I was briefly worried about it falling off. Me? Oh, shit.

"Michael, what the hell are you talking about? You left me, remember? And you broke my heart when you did it."

"I know, and I'm so sorry. It was the worst mistake of my life. I never should have left you."

"So, why did you then? And why did you cheat on me with Charlotte?"

He winced. "You figured that out, huh?"

"Michael, I'm not an idiot. I figured that out months ago. What I want to know is why? And why did you come back here now, declaring yourself to me when I'm engaged to be married? I'm happy, you moron. You can't just come back in here like you never left and take me back."

"Catie, I really made a mistake. And I know who I want now. I was so foolish for ever leaving you."

"Yeah, you were. But it's ok. I love Ryan. He's a wonderful man and he's finally made me happy. Michael, I realized a lot of things over the past year. Our relationship wasn't healthy."

He frowned at that. "It was fine. We just had some issues to work out."

"No, if it had been worth it, we would have worked them out. But we both let it go. We didn't try to make it work because it wasn't worth saving. You and I were conveniences to each other. I don't want to be anyone's convenience. I want to be someone's love, and now I am."

"But Catie, I can provide better for you and I won't saddle you with some kid that isn't yours."

"Do you honestly think I'm saddled with anything? I love Benjie. He's my family. We are a family, all three of us. I'm not going to throw that away for something that belongs in the past or for money."

"But I can do better for you. And besides, I know you so well."

"No, you know the old me. I'm a brand-new person, and I'm happy."

"Damn it, Catie. Why are you being so stubborn?"

"Because I'm happy. Now. Without you. I love Ryan, you dumbass. When you left me, you crushed me. But I got up again and I have a new life."

"You don't know what you're saying. We had a great life once. We could have that again, you know."

"What happened to me being a child and you not wanting to take care of me?"

"I made a mistake, ok? Can't you forgive me? Why are you so willing to throw away all that history?"

"Because the past is the past and the future is where I'm looking. You have no idea how much I've grown. Michael, I think you should go now, before I decide to karate-chop you."

He stood up.

"Fine, but I'll be back."

"Thanks for the warning. I'll be sure to be gone when you get here."

He walked to the door but, at the last minute, he spun and grabbed me, enfolding me in a steel embrace. I wasn't prepared for his unexpected attack. His lips crushed mine in a violent, passionate kiss that would have melted my heart a year ago. Now it just made me angry. I pushed against him with all my might but he simply wrapped his arms tighter around me and held me close, assaulting me with his mouth. I squealed and struggled against him.

"What the fuck is going on here?" an angry voice blasted from the doorway.

Michael jumped and released me but not before caressing my back and trailing his hand down my spine. I raced to Ryan's side and said, "I can explain."

"I bet you can. What the hell are you doing here, you asshole?"

"I was just leaving," Michael said, smirking. "I'll see you later, honey."

He walked out the door, a swagger in his step that infuriated me. He knew exactly what he was doing and how it would look to Ryan.

"Do you mind explaining to me what that dickhead was doing with his hands and his lips all over you?" Ryan asked coldly, his eyes distant and hurt.

"Ryan, it's not what you think."

"Yeah, it never is. You know, Nancy said the same thing when I caught her making out with her boyfriend in our house. I came home early that night to surprise her, too. It figures. You women are all the same."

"What the hell are you talking about? I wasn't doing anything. He came here to tell me he still loved me and I told him to jump off a cliff. Why aren't you listening to me?"

I felt like I had been slapped in the face. How dare he accuse me of cheating on him? Didn't he know anything about me?

"Yeah, you looked like you told him to jump off a cliff. I've heard that line before. Why don't you just get out? Go stay with your precious boyfriend."

"Ryan, you don't know what you're saying. He's not my boyfriend. If you'd just let me explain to you what happened, you'd understand," I pleaded with him, panic filling my heart, tears filling my eyes.

"That's what they all say when they get caught. Well, I don't need this shit. I'm not going through this again. Just go. Get out."

"Ryan, I'm not Nancy. Not all women are out to screw you over. I thought you knew me better than that."

He turned his back to me, arms folded across his chest. "Just leave. Now, damn it!"

He roared that last line, catapulting me into action. I went into our bedroom, flung open the closet door and grabbed an armload of clothing. I stuffed it into a duffle bag and stormed into the bathroom. I loaded up my toiletries and zipped the bag closed. I hefted the bag onto my shoulder and walked toward the door, every muscle in my body aching to wrap my arms around Ryan and make him see what he was doing. But he was still facing away from me, staring at the wall, his shoulders square and rigid. There was no talking to him.

Before I left, I leaned against the door frame, and said, "I love you, you know. Nothing will change that. I just think you have some things to work out before you're really ready to love me back. I'll miss you, but I'll be waiting."

I gently closed the door and walked to my car. I drove to the first place I could think of—my childhood home.

Gran's house was all lit up and there were three or four cars in the driveway. It appeared that I was about to interrupt one of her famous dinner parties. Funny that I hadn't been invited.

I opened the front door and walked into the formal dining room. Sure enough, eight people dressed to the nines were seated around the massive cherry dining table, forks poised to consume Gran's elegant offerings.

She glanced up as I came into the room, and shock and irritation darted across her face before she smoothly hid it and said, "My granddaughter, Caitlin, who apparently forgot her manners."

"Hi, everyone. Gran, can I talk to you?"

"Not now, Caitlin. Why don't you come back tomorrow?"

"Gran," I ground out through gritted teeth. "I have something I kind of need to discuss with you now."

"Catie, I'm in the middle of a very important dinner. Can't this wait?"

"No, Gran. It can't. Why the hell did you give Michael directions to my apartment?"

I saw a smirk cross Gran's face before she carefully masked it with a look of innocence.

"Oh, did Michael stop by?"

"You know damn well he did. And he tried to put the moves on me. And then Ryan threw me out because of it. Why would you tell Michael where I lived? Did you know he was planning on coming to my house to try to get me back? Why the hell would you do that?"

The silk-clad dinner guests that Gran was entertaining hung on to every word of our exchange. To the gossipy high-brows that Gran socialized with, this was the entertainment of the century.

"I don't know what you're talking about. It's not my fault that Ryan caught you in a compromising position," she sniffed delicately.

"Compromising position? You have got to be kidding me. Well, thanks to you and your helpful directions, I'm homeless. Can I stay in my old room for a few days until I can figure this out?"

"I'd rather you didn't, Caitlin. You know how I feel, and the timing isn't convenient."

"So you'd throw me out in the cold because the timing doesn't suit you? Why, you selfish old bitch!" I hollered at the top of my lungs. How dare she send me away because it wasn't convenient for her? Where the hell else was I supposed to go?

"I cannot believe you'd use that tone with your grandmother, and in front of all of my friends, too. I raised you better than that, even though you apparently have the morals of an alley cat."

"Actually, you didn't. You ignored me or disapproved of everything I did. You looked down your nose at me at every chance you'd get and you blamed me for my parents' death. You all but forced me out of the house when I turned eighteen, then had the nerve to complain about it when I moved in with Michael. And now where am I supposed to go? You knew this would happen, didn't you, you vindictive bitch? And you didn't care. And why the hell then are you still referring to yourself as my grandmother? We both know how you feel."

I stormed over to her chair and glowered down at her, rage snapping in my eyes. She gasped, and her face reddened. The people at the table were shocked too, but they were enjoying themselves.

"Caitlin, I think you should leave."

"Yeah, that seems to be the going trend tonight. I'm leaving and I will not be back. You've neglected me for the last time. You hear me? I'm gone. I'm dead. Forget about me. Live in this tomb with the ghost of my mother and enjoy the rest of your bitter life. You blew it, Gran. I'm not going to take your shit anymore. You didn't want me in your life? Well, you finally got your wish."

I turned on my heel and walked out of Gran's life.

I would not go back. I had learned in the last year that sometimes you have to let things go. She had obviously let me go years ago and it was pointless to hold on.

I recalled the way Ryan looked as I left and swallowed a sob. He was so hurt, and for nothing. If he had only listened to me when I tried to explain, none of this would have happened. And I never really realized that he was still harboring so many insecurities about women. Ryan's happiness had been shattered by a conniving in-law who didn't think he was good enough to be part of their family. And tonight he walked into what appeared to be the same exact scene. Who wouldn't be upset?

After all, from our first 'date', I rejected the idea of being with him. I made it exceedingly difficult for him to get close to me. I resisted our relationship and it wasn't until after Michael announced his engagement that I was able to break free from the need I had for him. How would that have looked to Ryan? He probably considered himself my second choice. He had already been someone else's second choice. Damn it.

I drove around town aimlessly. I wasn't sure where to go. It was obvious that I couldn't go back to Ryan's apartment. He didn't want me there. The thought of going to Kelly's explosion-in-a-Chinese-laundry apartment was scary, and I didn't want to go to Heidi's place either. She probably had some homeless person she had taken in bunked there.

Instead, I drove to Isamu's house. I was always welcome there. He answered the door in his bathrobe. I glanced at my watch and groaned. It was late and I had probably awoken him.

"Catie, what is the matter? Is Ryan alright?"

I sighed. "Isamu, nothing is alright. Can I stay here for a while?"

He opened the door wider. "Of course you can, Daughter. Now tell me, what happened?"

I trudged to his living room and flopped down on his comfortable sofa. Isamu loved all things American and his living room was a sumptuous collection of deep leather couches and gleaming wood.

I told him everything that transpired. He sat silently through my story, deep in concentration. When I finally finished, I was drained but relieved to have been able to talk it out without interruption.

"Catie, adversity is the foundation of virtue."

"Well, I should be very virtuous by now."

"You are. Do you not see that?"

"Not really. I just thought that I was living my life, and getting stomped on at every opportunity."

"Catie, you have overcome many obstacles. You have learned how to be but, more importantly, you have learned how not to be."

I mulled this in my head. I knew Isamu was right. I knew for certain I didn't want to be as cold, vindictive and unloving as my Gran. I knew that I didn't want to be as untrusting as Ryan was. And I knew I didn't want my loyalties to be as easily swayed as Michael's. Huh. I'll be darned—I had learned a lesson.

"But what do I do about Ryan? Isamu, I love him so much."

"He will also need to learn how he does not want to be. In time I think he will figure it out. But for now he will require some space."

"I hope you're right."

"Isamu is always right. Now, how about some pasta?"

Chapter 21

I knew Ryan needed time. I knew he was distrustful and hurt and angry. I knew he had things he needed to work out, but damn it, I wished he would hurry up with it!

It had been a month since our stormy last night together and I was getting impatient. I tried to meditate often to calm myself and give myself patience, but it was getting harder and harder to wait for him to come to me. I knew he had to come to me. I went out with Kelly and Heidi often, and although they respected the fact that I still considered myself engaged, they had been trying lately to introduce me to their single guy friends. I wasn't interested at all. I wanted my man back and the wait was excruciating.

I sparred with Bradley Shaw a lot, working out all of my excess frustration that the meditation couldn't erase, but he was starting to complain that I was hitting too hard. After his second black eye and third bloody nose, he wore pads and just let me whale on him. Although I wasn't exercising the control that Isamu had taught me, at least I felt much better afterward.

I hadn't talked to Gran. I refused to call her and I knew she was too proud to call me. She was probably still pissed that I ruined her party and exposed her true personality to all of her friends. Isamu cautioned me not to completely write off the only family I had left, but I argued that he was more closely related to me than she was. Being a family meant unconditionally accepting and supporting your loved ones, no matter what choices they made. Gran was incapable of doing that. Actually, I felt better without her constant negative influence. Without her nastiness in my life, I felt surprisingly peaceful.

The peace crossed into other aspects of my life as well. My job was going very well and my little patients were progressing by leaps and bounds. It seemed that once I accepted the direction my life was going, things started falling into place.

Still, I missed Ryan. He was the man of my dreams, even if I had realized it too late. It went against every fiber in my being to let him come to me. I was so used to fighting for what I wanted. Not being able to fight was like not being able to breathe.

I constantly wondered what he was doing and how he was faring with his ghosts. Had he exorcised them yet? Would he? Or would he hole himself up with his bitterness like my Gran did?

While I waited, another month had passed and winter came upon us like a vicious animal, hard and fast. Before the end of November snow blanketed the ground and turned our vibrant city into a colorless, somber anathema. Life slowed down. The air was harsh and bitter, and most people hunkered down to await fairer climes. Isamu and I were no different. We sat at home most nights, playing board games and reading, trying to ease the ennui of the season. I felt safe and secure with my surrogate dad but I longed to feel Ryan's arms around me again.

One day, about a week before Christmas, I drove to work like I normally did and walked into the break room to hang up my coat. Megan was in there when I entered, and she nodded and smiled to me. Sallie had quit her job two months ago and the office gossip had died down. Megan had proven to be a nice woman when she wasn't under Sallie's negative influence. I murmured a quick, "Good morning," and hung up my heavy winter coat. She returned the greeting and said, "Did you have a look at your patient line-up for the day?"

"No, not yet. Why?" I asked curiously.

"You may recognize one of your patients," Megan said gently.

"Oh, not little Roger Madigan? Did he fall off his skateboard again?" I groaned. Roger was a handful, and he'd already broken his right ankle, his left arm and his right leg in various sports-related accidents.

"No, not him. Honey, you may want to sit down."

I frowned. "What's going on, Megan?"

"I put together a chart for a Benjamin Ashford today. He broke his leg in three places."

I gasped. Benjie? Not sweet little Benjie! "Oh, my God! What happened?"

"The chart said he fell down some stairs at his mom's house. Are you going to be able to handle this?"

"Of course I am. That's my son—I mean, Ryan's son. I'll be fine." I was shaking. Little Benjie was hurt and my heart ached for him. I pictured the sweet little mop-top and my eyes misted. I missed him so much, just as much as I missed his father. "When is he scheduled to come in?"

"This morning. He's six weeks into the break and the orthopedic surgeon said he should start working on mobility and strength."

"I see. Megan, thanks for telling me. Can I have a minute?"

Megan left and I sat down at the break room table, my head in my hands. Poor Benjie. And poor Ryan. He must be beside himself with worry.

I was glad they were coming to see me but I was concerned about how Benjie would feel once he saw me. We hadn't seen each other since Ryan walked in on the scene with Michael and he must be so upset about my unexpected absence from his life. I wondered what Ryan had told him. No matter what, I had to maintain a professional distance. Hard as that would be, it was the only way. There was no sense in giving Benjie (or myself) false hope.

I glanced at my schedule and saw that Benjie was my first patient of the day. I reviewed his chart and gathered everything I would need to help him regain mobility and strength in his leg. After six weeks in a cast, his leg was sure to be atrophied and it would be slow going to get him back to his original shape.

At precisely 9:00, Benjie and his dad arrived at the office. Megan checked them in and directed them to my room. It was a large, bright space filled with fun things like large exercise balls, steps to nowhere and colorful rugs. A miniscule primary-colored light-up treadmill graced one wall and colorful blocks that patients picked up, stepped on or jumped from were strewn around the room. Elastic bands in various wild shades hung from wooden pegs on my walls and colorful art was plastered everywhere. It looked like the inside of a crayon box. Kids loved it. I tried to make their therapy fun, and for a time, while they hooted and hollered and jumped and played, they forgot about the pain.

Benjie entered my room on crutches. He was doing quite well and I was proud of him for mastering such a difficult means of walking. His tongue was between his teeth and I could see him chewing on it in concentration, but as soon as he looked up and saw me, he squealed and pumped his little arms even harder in order to reach me faster.

"Catie! I missed you! Guess what? I broke my leg. It hurt bad. What are you doing here?" He dropped his crutches and flung himself into my arms.

"Benjie!" I gave him a squeeze. "I'm here to get your leg feeling better." I leaned back so I could look at him. "So, what happened?"

"Oh, I just fell down some stairs."

"I see that. You poor kid. Well, we'll get you walking right again in no time, ok?"

"Ok."

I glanced at Ryan but he refused to look at me. His gaze traveled around the room, taking in the colorful equipment curiously. I wondered if he was impressed by my room. He had never seen what I did before and, although I was sad that his first visit was because of his son, I was proud to show off what I could do.

I decided to break the ice.

"Hi," I murmured.

"Hi."

"How are you?"

"Fine, thank you." As polite as a church elder, I grumbled to myself. Damn stubborn man!

"Well, we'll get Benjie back in shape soon."

For the next hour, I guided Benjie through some mobility exercises. We worked his leg up and down, from side to side, and flexed his little foot to work his calf muscle. He winced several times, causing his father to wince too, but handled his therapy like a little trooper. I made notes in his chart and took baseline measurements of his mobility. I watched Ryan as much as I watched Benjie, hoping for a glance, a smile, something. My gaze was met with stone. Ryan was rigid, stiff and utterly unforgiving. So he wasn't going to forget my supposed transgressions? Well, fine, but I would give his son my all, a last gift to the man I loved before I counted him out forever.

When our session was over, Benjie gave me a huge hug and said, "That was fun, Catie. Do I get to come back to see you again?"

I returned his exuberant hug and assured him, "Sure do. How's Wednesday?"

He giggled and said, "I don't know. You'll have to ask my daddy."

I glanced at Ryan, only to see him glancing at me. I asked quietly, "Wednesday?"

"Should be fine. I'll check my schedule."

"Great. Go talk to Anna up front. She'll set you up."

As they left, I was sure that my heart walked out the door with them. I passed the rest of the day in a fog. Megan tried to ask me how it went. I merely grunted and walked past her with a blank look on my face.

When I got home, Isamu was waiting with some chicken parmesan. Eenie, Meeney, and Miney were all lined up, panting and drooling in anticipation of their upcoming meal. I threw my coat on the back of the sofa, trudged into the kitchen and heaved myself into a chair.

"Was it a rough day today, Daughter?" Isamu asked me, a wry grin crossing his face.

"You might say that. Benjie was there."

"As a patient?"

"Yeah. He broke his leg. Ryan brought him to therapy today."

"Really? And how is Ryan doing?"

I snarled quietly, "I don't know. He barely looked at me."

"Give him time, Daughter. He will see the light of day eventually."

"Yeah, but until then, we're both miserable. You should've seen the look on his face." I attacked my chicken with fervor. It smelled delicious, and all of the pent-up anger and loneliness I felt converted itself to hunger.

"Love is patient and kind," Isamu chastised me.

"Yeah, I know. I'll be patient and kind when I get him back," I grumbled. I wasn't in the mood for proverbs, Japanese or otherwise.

On Wednesday, Ryan and Benjie came back, and Benjie was just as happy to see me as he was before. He threw his arms around me and said, "I missed you, Catie. I was worried I wouldn't be able to see you again."

"Of course you will, Benjie, my man. We still have a lot of work to do to get your leg back to normal. Have you been practicing what I showed you at home?"

He nodded solemnly.

"Good, show me what you've been doing." I nodded as he went through the exercises I showed him during our first session. I was pleased to note a little progress. His mobility was already improving. Kids are amazingly flexible and quick to heal. Soon we'd be able to work on getting his strength back.

"Ok, Benjie. Here's what we'll be doing today." I guided him through some simple stretches with my colorful rubber bands and soon he was using them on his own, using his leg muscles to stretch the bands left and right and back again. I propped myself against the wall and watched him clinically, shouting out encouragement here and there, and praising him time and again as he stretched further, further. He was really amazing and I was as proud of him as I would have been had he been my own son.

Ryan stood by and watched, occasionally offering his own words of praise. He glanced at me periodically and I could tell that he wanted to say more than he did. I think he was torn, however. After all, this was my job. How much could he say? I was acting in my professional capacity, and he was out of his league seeing me at work this way. I wasn't just his ex-fiancée. I was his son's health care provider. I could feel the tension in the room as clearly as I could feel a warm summer breeze. I felt for him, truly I did, but part of me was angry. After all, he was the one who forced our break-up. If he had let me explain what had happened between me and Michael, we'd be going through this together right now and not standing apart like strangers.

The session ended way too soon and I scheduled Benjie to come back again on Friday. Until his leg completely healed, it was important that I see him three times per week. I worried that Ryan thought I was milking the appointments to get close to him but shrugged it off. I was acting in Benjie's best interests. If Ryan couldn't accept that, he could go climb a tree and fall out for all I cared, and I wouldn't even provide therapy for the stubborn ass.

Each time I saw Ryan, I went home and moaned to Isamu about my plight. It was a sweet torture to see Ryan and Benjie three times a week. I longed to gather them both into my arms and never let go. God, how I missed that stubborn man. I wanted to go back to Ryan's apartment. It was home. I wanted my happiness back. Seeing them, while it was amazing, was just a tease.

Isamu tried to comfort me. "You must be patient, Catie. Things will work out in the end."

"I hope you're right. I'm getting tired of waiting," I told him.

"Rome wasn't built in a day."

"That's not a Japanese proverb."

"No, but it fits."

I shrugged. It did fit. Damn those Romans and their slow architecture. Still, some things were worth waiting for and I could be patient as the day was long.

Christmas was lonely. I always hated it anyway, ever since my parents died, and Gran and I weren't on speaking terms anymore. Even though I suspected her absence from my life was the greatest gift I could have received from her, it was still different. Normally I went to Gran's house every Christmas Eve for a black-tie dinner. This year, Isamu and I gathered around his kitchen table and gorged ourselves on pasta primavera as we watched the dogs inhale their helpings without chewing.

It seemed like everything was changing. Heidi was over the moon with happiness due to her engagement to Peter and they had traveled to his native Oregon to be with his family for the holidays.

Kelly had dumped Camden for one of the attorneys at her office. She and her new beau, Scott, booked a Caribbean cruise for three weeks. I had already received two breathless phone calls and one postcard from her.

All in all it was a quiet Christmas and I wondered how different things would have been if I was at Ryan's apartment with him and Benjie. I was sure that it would have been much louder and more chaotic, what with all the cool electronic little boy toys that Benjie would have gotten from Santa.

I sighed wistfully. What I wouldn't have given to be there right now watching Benjie open his presents and squeal with delight.

Isamu nudged me gently. "Where were you just then, my daughter? Up in the clouds?"

"No, with my loved ones."

"And what am I?" he asked, smiling at me.

"You know what you are to me. But they are, too."

"I know. Someday you will be able to reclaim your family. Until then, you are welcome here with me."

I hugged him. If only someday were now.

New Year's Eve came and went uneventfully. Instead of making a resolution, I made a wish. I wished to be able to be with the ones I loved, with no strings attached, no duty involved. I wished to be with my loved ones because they wanted me to be there. I had been pensive as of late and I had come to several conclusions.

I was over the past. Truly I was. I had finally come to realize that life was a journey. We accepted that journey with our first breath, and we would continue it until our last. The rewards along the way made it worth taking. Even if we experienced loss, we had to plod on. I was reminded of the proverb, "The journey of a thousand miles begins with a single step." I wondered how many steps I had taken and how many more I had to go. And I wondered when Ryan would decide to come along. Our paths had veered in opposite directions. Would we ever find each other again?

I also thought of my adoptive parents. They loved me enough to take me in and make me a part of their family. No, things didn't end up the way any of us wanted, but they gave me the best ten years they could and I wouldn't trade them for anything. I spent a lot of time wondering about my birth parents but I decided that I wouldn't look for them, for a while at least. I had parents. Good ones. Still, I spent a lot of time thinking about them. I wondered if I looked like either of them. Did I have their eyes? Hair? Attitude? It blew my mind to think of it.

As far as Gran went, I pitied her. She was alone. Friends and social status were no substitute for family. And look at Isamu—he wasn't even related by marriage, yet he took me in and cared for me as though I was his own. His love for me had nothing to do with genes, but it was genuine and unshakeable. I felt the same way about Benjie. He wasn't mine but I loved him with all my heart. He meant the world to me and I hoped that someday his fool of a father would come to his senses and let me back into his life. Until then, I had only to wait and hope and pray that I'd get my wish.

The start of the New Year indicated the start of a new me. I was content with myself, something that I never felt before, and it was amazing. And maybe someday, I could live with the man of my dreams and a little boy who deserved the security of a family.

Chapter 22

After New Year's break, I went back to work with the rest of the staff at Dr. Ross's office. We all exchanged pleasantries and tales of holiday cheer, but after about ten minutes of that it was time to get back to work.

All day I worked with my little clients, goading and guiding them into rehabilitation with my own particular brand of encouragement. When Robbie Malloy came in to try his robotic arm for the first time, I told him he was more awesome than even Optimus Prime. He was most impressed. As Tanisha Gould took her first solo steps since the accident that crushed her feet, I called her 'Twinkle Toes' and promised her a new pair of shoes if she could walk twenty feet by next month. She grinned at me and did fifteen within her first thirty minutes of therapy. I wondered briefly how much a new pair of Sketchers with metallic trim would cost.

Benjie was scheduled as my last appointment of the day. He hobbled in without his crutches and I was overjoyed at his progress. Apparently, someone had been taking his therapy very seriously. Given what I knew of Ryan, however, I wasn't surprised. I knew he was supervising his son and encouraging him to give his therapy his best effort. Ryan was a fantastic dad and I knew how much that helped.

"Catie! Happy New Year!" Benjie shouted at me as he limped to me. He gave me an enthusiastic hug and smiled up at me.

"Look at you! You'll be back to karate kicks in no time if you keep this up. You know that?"

"I know. Daddy says that If I can get my leg better soon, he's gonna enroll me in Is… Isa… Isamanu's class."

"Do you mean Isamu?" I questioned him softly.

"Yeah, Isamu. I always mess that up. Do you know him?"

"I sure do, Benjie. He's like a daddy to me. Just like your daddy is to you. You'll like his dojo very much," I assured him.

What was Ryan doing? It seemed strange to me that Ryan would enroll Benjie in my sensei's class, especially considering he all but cast me aside. Wouldn't that have been weird for him?

"Cool. I bet he's real nice. Wanna see what I can do?" Benjie slowly took a step forward. He was concentrating so hard that he was chewing on his tongue again, something I'd seen him do countless times while he played video games. He walked approximately three yards before he swayed on his feet. Ryan and I rushed forward at the same time, both of us intent on catching our tiny buddy, and we met in the middle of the room, bumping each other. The contact was electric.

"Oh, sorry," I squealed.

I jumped and stepped to the side, allowing Ryan to rescue Benjie. Ryan glanced at me and as our eyes met, my heart stopped. I missed him so much. But I couldn't turn this therapy session into personal time. I looked at Ryan and asked, "Do you have him?"

He nodded thoughtfully and propped Benjie back up. Ryan handed him back his crutches and Benjie fit them back underneath his arms.

I smiled at him and ruffled his hair. "Good job, buddy. Now, let's get you over here to this red block. We're going to try some heel dips to get some strength back into your calf."

I stood Benjie up on the block with his heel stuck off the back. I showed him how to steady himself with his crutches and instructed him to dip his heel down off the block and balance on his toes to stretch his calf muscle and build up some strength. He was soon dipping and grinning.

"So, do you think he's coming along ok?" Ryan murmured. It was the first direct question Ryan asked me since the Benjie started therapy. I was startled and secretly thrilled to be able to converse with him again.

"Yes, I do. He's already regained a lot of his mobility, and strength will come. In time he'll be running around again."

"Good. That's good. I'm glad. I, uh, wanted to thank you for working with him. He's happy that you're the one taking care of him."

"I'm glad to be the one taking care of him. He's a great little guy." I dared to smile at him and I was surprised to see him smiling back, though very carefully.

"Yeah. He is."

"Ryan, can I ask how he … you know, how he hurt himself?" I had been very curious since he came on as my patient. Normally Benjie loved elevators and escalators, and the stairs in most buildings these days were for emergencies only.

"I'd rather not get into that now. It's a long story."

"Ok. No problem. Listen, he's pretty much done for the day, so, I guess I'll see you later on in the week?"

"Sure. Unless you'd like to go out for a bite to eat?" he asked hesitantly, almost as though he was afraid I'd say no.

My heart felt like it would leap from my chest but I got control of myself and replied levelly, "I'd like that. You guys are my last appointment. If you want to wait in the waiting room for a few minutes, I'll finish my charts and meet you out front?"

"Ok. We'll be waiting." He smiled shyly at me and called to Benjie, "Come on, my man. We're done."

"Ok, Daddy. See you, Catie."

I normally did all my chart notes before I left for the day, but tonight I rushed and jotted down only the basics. I dictated the rest and left the cassette for our transcriptionist to tackle. After all, I had a date with my men!

They were both waiting for me as I stepped into the waiting room. "Are you ready?" Ryan asked me. I nodded and he put his hand on the small of my back to guide me out the door. I wanted to cry, the contact was so sweet.

I hopped into his car and we drove to Pizzazz. The inviting pizza parlor brought back warm memories of my first date with Ryan and Benjie. We snagged the same table and, once again, Benjie patted the cushion next to where he was sitting. I sat down beside him and watched Ryan as he slid into the booth across from me. My heart stuttered in reaction to his fluid movements. His eyes pierced mine with an electric gaze and I knew at that moment that none of my love for him was lost during our separation. In fact, it seemed to have increased ten-fold. My heart bursting with it, I cautioned myself to go slowly. There was such a tentative feeling to this dinner, and I didn't dare rush things and destroy it.

"So, how have you been?" he asked me. He seemed concerned, and I wondered if he was worried that I had moved on.

"A little lonely. You?"

He colored and cleared his throat. At least he knew how I felt. As much as I wanted to leap into his arms and never let go, I forced myself to go slowly and allow him to set the pace for this reunion. The waitress came and we ordered our pizza quickly to get rid of any outside distractions.

"Really good. Benjie lives with me now." His chest puffed with pride and a jubilant smile burst forth from my lips.

"You had the custody hearing? What happened?" I couldn't believe it. I was so happy for them, yet sad that I wasn't there to see it.

"It's part of the long story, but here goes." He settled himself more comfortably in the booth and began.

"Nancy fought me hard and her high-priced lawyer tried every trick in the book to make things go their way. Andrew, her asshole husband, had already moved to the city to start work and she was left at home to care for Benjie. I guess it was more than she could handle. One night she had a little too much to drink and Benjie had a bad dream. He wanted his mom to cuddle him and comfort him. He came out into the living room to find her. She hollered at him to go back to bed and shoved him toward his room. He stumbled and went down the stairs."

I gasped and tears flooded my eyes. His own mother broke his leg?

"Child Protective Services called me and said he was in the emergency room with a possible fracture. I called my lawyer and he met me at the hospital. Benjie confirmed what happened and CPS awarded temporary protective custody to me. We went to court and the judge did something unheard of: he asked Benjie to testify."

"And?" I asked with baited breath.

"And he asked Benjie who he'd rather live with, and why. He said he'd rather live with his daddy because I never pushed him or swore at him or made him stay in his room when friends came to visit."

"Oh, Ryan," I murmured, so heartsick for the little boy who only wanted to be loved. And I was insanely happy that justice prevailed and the little boy was where he was wanted.

"He's with me for good. The judge ruled that Nancy could have him for two weeks in the summer, under supervision, in Pennsylvania. She's not allowed to leave the state with him."

"So you got what you wanted," I said quietly, reaching out and grasping his hand. I squeezed it gently.

He squeezed back and swallowed when he looked down at our joined hands and noticed the engagement ring he bought me, still on my finger.

"Not quite."

"Well, what's missing?" I asked him.

"You."

"But—"I protested. He had dumped me, so what was he saying?

"Catie, I was a fool. I should have listened to you."

"Why didn't you?" I asked.

"Well, for starters, I don't like to see my woman in a lip-lock with another man. It tends to cloud my judgment. And I was still reeling from my own divorce. I guess I wasn't ready to trust anyone yet when we first started dating. I was trying to help you through your issues without overcoming my own."

"I'm sorry. That certainly wasn't my intention," I sputtered.

"No, I didn't mean it that way. I just meant that I should have taken the time to clear my own mind before I got involved. Maybe then I wouldn't have jumped all over you for something that wasn't your fault."

I was about to speak when our pizza arrived. Benjie giggled in delight as the cheese from the piece that the waitress served to him stretched to an amazing length before landing on the table, leaving an edible trail from the pizza pan to his plate. He busied himself with his food and I peered at Ryan again. He was staring at me intently, leaning forward in the booth. He grabbed both of my hands in his and spoke again.

"Catie, you may not approve of what I'm going to tell you, but I have to do this. I have to tell you what happened and let you decide what you want to do."

"Uh, ok...," I stammered, at a loss for words. What was he talking about?

"I ran Michael's information through our police database and found an address for him. I went to his house and confronted him. He admitted that your Gran gave him directions to my apartment. Apparently he called the precinct and found out that I was getting out early. He knew exactly when to be at my house so that I'd be sure to walk in on you two in a compromising position."

"That's what I tried to tell you." I took his hand and squeezed it.

"That's not all. I punched him in the face, Catie. I'm sorry I did it. I couldn't help myself. He cost me the love of my life, and it pissed me off."

"You punched Michael?" I was shocked. My mild-mannered, even-tempered cop went up to someone and punched him in the face? Wow. I guessed he was a little pissed about the situation. I was slightly irritated, but only because I wish I had been there to see it.

"Yeah, but that's still not all." He looked at me sheepishly.

"Oh, God. What else did you do?" I wondered, anguished now.

"Well, when I pulled up his record, I found an old parking ticket that he forgot to pay. It appeared that his license was suspended. So, I told Danny. He wrote him a few tickets."

"He didn't!"

"Only about a thousand dollars' worth. He waited outside Michael's apartment until he saw him get in his car, then followed him for a few blocks and pulled him over."

"I bet he was pissed."

"Well, yeah, but when Danny threatened to impound his car instead, he got real polite about the whole thing."

"No, there's no abuse of power in the police department, is there?" I teased him.

"When someone messes with the woman I want to marry, I get even. End of story. So do you still want to? Get married?"

My heart thundered. The answer to that question would determine how the rest of my life would go. "With all my heart."

He leaned forward and kissed my lips softly, tenderly.

Benjie looked up from his pizza in time to see our kiss and said, "Ewww. Not while I'm eating, you guys."

We all giggled and I hugged the precious boy to my heart. He would know love, security and comfort for the rest of his life. And so would I.

Chapter 23

Planning our wedding was easy; after all, I already had everything I needed. We ended up setting a date in late spring and I feverishly worked to get everything finalized. I continued to stay at Isamu's house for the duration of my engagement. I decided I wanted to do things right and Isamu was thrilled to be part of my plans. He was looking forward to walking me down the aisle, and he told me time and again that he had a special surprise for me. As easy as it usually was for me to pry information from him, this time was different. His lips were sealed.

Gran was invited to the wedding but she declined the invitation. Maybe one day she'd come around, and maybe she wouldn't. But either way, I wouldn't let her selfishness get in the way of my happiness.

The morning of my wedding was hectic. I raced to meet Heidi and Kelly at our favorite salon for hair, nails and makeup. Afterward, we were to jet over to the church for pictures and last-minute preparations. My girls met me at the salon with a bottle of champagne and we got silly on bubbly as our stylists made us nuptial-chic. I gathered both of them close to me and said, "You two are the best friends a girl could have, you know that?"

"Sure, I bet you say that to all of the people who suggest you go find a one-night stand," Heidi giggled. I was struck dumb by her words. That seemed like it was so long ago and here I was, about to be married to the man I seduced in a bar.

I hugged her impulsively. "Oh, Heidi, I owe this all to you. You know that? I probably never would have met Ryan if it hadn't been for your stupid magazine article."

Kelly laughed. "Sure you would. I know how fast you drive. It was just a matter of time before he pulled you over for speeding."

Heidi smiled. "And I would probably still be a virgin if it hadn't been for your bad influence on me."

My jaw hit the floor. "You didn't."

"Yep, sure did. And with the man of your dreams, it doesn't seem like a sin at all, even before marriage."

Kelly snorted. "I could have told you that a long time ago."

"Yeah, but I had more fun finding out on my own. Did you know that the reverse cowgirl is really quite amazing? I had no idea."

I rolled my eyes and chugged my champagne. This was why I didn't engage in girl-talk.

We reached the church about two hours before the wedding. We were immediately whisked away into one of the anterooms to get changed into our finery. Heidi and Kelly carefully pulled my dress over my head and smoothed it down my body. They cooed and sighed and told me I looked like a princess. I smiled. Even though I was more at home in my blue jeans, I was glad that I looked like a fairy tale today. This was the real first day of the rest of my life. I felt that the occasion called for a little luxury and glamour.

A knock on the door sounded and in rushed Benjie, adorable in his black tux and white cummerbund.

"Gosh, you look pretty, Catie. Daddy says that it's almost time to get married. He wants to know if you're alright. I'm s'posed to go tell him."

"Oh, my sweet Benjie, I love you. You look terrific. Tell him I'm wonderful, ok?"

"Ok. I love you too. Bye, Catie!" he said as he galloped from the room. I chuckled as I watched him leave. His leg was completely healed and his chipper little attitude was intact. He came through the storm with flying colors, and Ryan and I had no doubt that it would be smooth sailing ahead for all three of us.

Minutes later, another knock sounded at the door. Kelly answered it and Isamu, resplendent in his own tux, came in. "Are you almost ready, Daughter?"

"I've been waiting for this day forever. I'm ready."

I beamed at him. He walked to my side and hugged me hard. He was almost as excited as I was about the wedding, and I wondered again about the surprise he promised me.

As if on cue, he said, "Catie, I have your surprise all ready. Would you like it now?"

"Of course I would. I can't believe you kept it a secret for this long," I giggled at him.

"I'll be right back." He squeezed me and kissed my brow. He turned and left. I wandered around the room and waited for him to come back, curiosity all but killing me. Whatever it was, it was big.

Isamu came back into the room and said, "Catie, my daughter, I have this for you." He held out an envelope.

"What is this? Are you writing me letters, Isamu?"

"No, my dear. Catie, this is from Maria DiCarlo. She is your birth mother."

I backed up into a chair and sat heavily. My birth mother? Oh my God. Wow.

I opened the envelope and removed a folded piece of stationary. A photo fell out of the center of the letter and I got my first glimpse of the woman who was my mother. She was tall, willowy and slender. Her violet eyes sparkled even in the photo and her dark hair, streaked with only a touch of grey, hung free to her shoulders. I stared, mouth agape. It was like I was looking into a mirror that saw ahead twenty years.

I opened the letter and began to read.

"Caitlin, I hope this letter doesn't cause you any pain. Isamu found me and told me that you were to be married today, and I had to write to you. I want you to know that not a day has gone by since I gave you up that I haven't thought about you, wondered about you. In my heart, we were together, and I hope that one day I can meet you and tell you all the things I have been saving for the first time I met you. Until then, just know that I love you, and I wish you all the best on your wedding day and all your days to come. Love, Maria."

I sniffed back happy tears and motioned Isamu into my arms for a hug. "I can't believe you did this."

He returned the hug and said, "Daughter, I wanted you to know the love of two parents on your wedding day. Your mother loves you. She wanted to come but worried that it was too soon. She did not want to ruin your special day."

"Do you think I'll really ever meet her?"

"I can guarantee it, if you wish it. She really is a remarkable woman and you are very much like her, in both appearance and action."

I pondered that statement in awe. Somewhere out there was

someone who looked like me, who acted like me, who was actually a part of me. It was humbling and mind-blowing. My heart overflowed.

Before I could quiz Isamu further on my newly-discovered family, Benjie charged into the room to tell us it was time. I took a deep breath and went to give my heart, my life, my very soul, to my man.

I felt overwhelmingly happy. My life was finally complete. I had family, friends and a man who loved me waiting at the end of an aisle to make me his wife. My whole future was ahead of me and I wouldn't look back, at least not too often. And when I did, I would be reminded only of my incredible journey and how far I had come.

As I walked down the aisle to Ryan, my eyes stung with happy tears and I silently thanked Kelly for forcing me to wear waterproof mascara. I met my groom at the front of the church and, as our eyes met, I was struck anew at how lucky I was.

"Hi," he whispered.

"Hi," I whispered back.

"Happy wedding day," he said, grasping my hands and squeezing gently.

"To you too," I replied, smiling at him through my tears.

"I love you with all my heart, always and forever."

"I love you too."

Pastor Robert Smith spoke of love, commitment and trust. The words may as well have been written specifically for us, they rang so true.

Finally, we sealed our vows with a kiss, and we were home.